LEO

LIGHTHOUSE SECURITY INVESTIGATIONS WEST COAST

MARYANN JORDAN

Cover: Graphics by Stacy

ISBN ebook: 978-1-956588-09-5

ISBN print: 978-1-956588-10-1

❀ Created with Vellum

Author's Note

Please remember that this is a work of fiction. I have lived in numerous states as well as overseas, but for the last thirty years have called Virginia my home. I often choose to use fictional city names with some geographical accuracies.

These fictionally named cities allow me to use my creativity and not feel constricted by attempting to accurately portray the areas.

It is my hope that my readers will allow me this creative license and understand my fictional world.

I also do quite a bit of research on my books and try to write on subjects with accuracy. There will always be points where creative license will be used in order to create scenes or plots.

1

Six Years Ago

"Come on, Leo. You know you want to. Hell, you'd probably give up your next leave to get balls deep into her."

Lionel Parker easily pulled his gaze away from the blonde on the dance floor as she looked over her shoulder toward him while shaking her bountiful assets. Instead of being dragged in by the woman's overt invitation to join her, he glanced at the woman sitting on the barstool next to him and grinned. Her long, dark hair hung over her shoulders, the tresses now wavy since being loosened from her usual tight regulation bun. Her barely-there makeup enhanced her dark brown eyes but wasn't needed to make her more beautiful. Faded jeans fit the curves of her hips but did little to add the illusion of height to her petite frame.

In fact, her feet were encased in her shit-kicker boots. When teased about being short, she'd always bark the same response. "Why the fuck would I want to teeter in heels that would hinder my ability to kick ass if a bar fight breaks out?"

He'd grown used to the typical black color of her tops. The wide neck hung off one shoulder, exposing her navy-blue tank underneath. She proclaimed that wearing black allowed her to be equally noticed while sitting on a barstool or hidden in the shadows, depending on her mood.

There was no doubt about it— Natalie Robinson was gorgeous. And as one of his team members, she was completely off-limits. As part of his support team, he needed her to be dedicated and focused, not pissed off or full of emotions that could get in the way of keeping him and the members of his Delta team safe. Not that he'd consider going there anyway. *Not with Natalie.* She'd become one of his best friends, and he wasn't about to fuck up that relationship.

"Is Lion on the prowl?" Rocker asked, hefting his muscular frame onto the barstool across from them. His call sign came from when he rocked back too far in his chair during an early training session, and the instructor kicked him the rest of the way over, causing the large man to splatter onto the floor.

Rolling his eyes, Leo took another swig of beer, then shook his head. His team members used his call sign, Lion, but off duty, Natalie had always used the name he'd given when he was first introduced to her. "Nah, more like Nat is just busting my balls."

"Aw, you're not afraid of our little Nat." Rocker reached out to place his large hand on top of Natalie's head but missed as she ducked out of the way.

"Touch my hair and lose your trigger finger, Rock," she said, her voice deadly serious while her eyes sparkled.

Rocker hesitated as the other team members at the table laughed. Leo knew that while they found her amusing, none of them were truly sure if she was serious or not. They'd all witnessed her take down big men on the dance floor for getting too handsy and laughed their asses off when she did.

"You better watch it," Leo warned, lifting a brow and stifling a grin. "You know she'd do it."

"Hell, yeah," Casper added. The quietest, most invisible team member seemed more like a ghost than a human but had witnessed Natalie's ability to handle herself enough to earn everyone's respect.

Discretion being the better part of valor, Rocker wiggled his fingers before pulling his hand back and twisting around to check out the blonde bombshell still gyrating on the dance floor. "Damn, if you're not going to sample what she's offering, I'm gonna get in there."

Lifting his beer bottle in a mock salute, Leo nodded. "Go for it."

The words had barely left his mouth before Rocker bolted from his stool and headed straight toward her.

Nat speared Leo with an intense gaze, both brows lifted. "Seriously, Leo? You let an easy lay like that slip through your fingers? Hell, her IQ might've even been higher than her boob measurements."

"Well, in case it wasn't, Rocker won't care."

Her lips quirked upward as she lost the battle not to show her amusement, something he noticed easily. Not surprising, since he noticed everything about her.

With the blonde no longer trying to capture his attention, Natalie sighed and shook her head. "Okay, let's see who else I can line up for you."

"What about you? I don't see you going after anybody."

"Fuck, man. This bar is filled with men I work with or wannabes." She sighed heavily, her mouth pursed. "And neither category does a thing for me."

He knew what she meant. The bar was close to Fort Bragg and filled with Army men and women. Leo's squadron was 1st Special Forces Operational Detachment - Delta, but while SFOD-D was official, they were now known as Army Compartmented Elements. But the elite members of the ACE stayed below the radar, even amongst those on base. Natalie wasn't about to date another ACE, but she had no interest in the other military or civilian wannabe pretenders. It wasn't the first time he'd realized her position as a female intelligence and logistics operator on their support team made hookups difficult. She was smart as hell, sharp as a tack, and Army strong.

Glancing around the bar, he knew most of the men there couldn't hold a candle to her. He also knew every member of the ACE squadrons would take a bullet for her, knowing she would do the same for them. Women were not members of Deltas, but as a support member, she was essential. As his gaze landed back on her, he had no problem admitting she was also invaluable to him as a best friend. "Maybe you're just not looking hard enough. There's gotta be a man here who would be worth taking home for a night's rodeo."

"You think I need practice on my reverse cowboy?"

Casper snorted as Leo barked out laughter. "Fuck, Nat. I don't reckon you need practice on anything."

She winked and grinned. "Damn straight."

"Maybe all these potentials are just intimidated by us hanging out with you," Baker quipped, sliding onto the stool that Rocker had abandoned. Tom Kupka had a drill sergeant that kept calling him Cupcake, but by the time he'd graduated from Operator Training Course, he gratefully accepted the call sign of Baker instead. Of course, once Natalie heard that story, she delighted in making sure he never forgot his earlier name.

"I can't imagine why any man would be intimidated by you, Cupcake," she threw out, slapping her hand against his shoulder. "Anyway, why would I want to go out with a man who's intimidated by other men?"

"Atta girl, Nat." Leo grinned, lifting his beer again. "You keep your standards high."

"If she keeps her standards that high, she'll never have a good romp." Casper's attention was quickly diverted by a woman rubbing her fingers along his shoulders when she approached.

Tossing back the rest of her beer, Natalie hopped down from the tall barstool. Looking up at him from her five-foot-four-inch height, she said, "All right, Leo, I'm out of here. You're on your own to find your true love for the night, and I'm going to go to a bar farther away from the base to see if I've got any chance of giving my vibrator a night off and knocking boots with a real man."

His brows snapped together. "I'll go with you."

"Jesus, the last thing I need is a babysitter or someone who intimidates the fuck out of a potential fuck." Grinning, she turned to walk away, then looked over her shoulder and winked. "Come over tomorrow afternoon. You bring the pizza, and I'll have the beer. We can either brag about our conquests or commiserate on the lack of good action. Plus, there's a game on at four."

With that, she pushed her way through the crowd, and he grinned. Her stature never hindered her ability to command attention. His gaze followed her until she was out the door, the desire to go with her filling his mind. While there was no way he could be the one she entertained for the night, that didn't mean he didn't feel it in his gut every time she left with someone else. Swiping his hand over his face, he tried to wipe the grimace off as well.

"I thought your little friend would never leave." The sultry voice came from the side, drawing his attention to the brunette with the fiery-red highlights who'd approached. "I'm Gerrie."

Her makeup was a little too heavy. Her top was a little too low. But with Natalie gone, taking away the easy conversation he always enjoyed with her, he had no reason to refuse this woman's attention. Not in the mood for an attempt at witty banter that would probably bore him silly, he stood and grabbed her hand. "Wanna dance?"

"I've got a place near here," Gerrie said. "I think I'd rather go there to *dance* instead."

He looked over her head and caught the eye of their server, lifting his chin. Tossing several bills onto the table that would cover his drinks, he looked back at Gerrie. Nothing about her was remarkable, but he wasn't looking for anything other than what she offered —a little no-strings fun. "Then lead the way," he said, noting the flash of confidence in her eyes as though his acceptance of her proposition was inevitable. Making his way through the bar, he couldn't understand why that bothered him so much. Stepping outside, her arms snaked around his waist, but his gaze scanned the parking lot, looking for and finding Natalie's small SUV as it pulled onto the street.

"What are you waiting for, soldier?"

He glanced down and observed the tip of her tongue dragging along her bottom lip in an over-exaggerated, coy, sultry move. Swallowing his sigh, he shook his head. "Not a thing. Let's go." Even as the words left his mouth, he knew they were a lie. What he was really waiting for was the next day's plans of beer, pizza, a game, and kicking back with his best friend.

2

FOUR YEARS AGO

"Tango approaching from the northwest," Natalie called out, her calm voice belying the adrenaline pumping through her bloodstream. She didn't need to look toward the ACE support team's radio controller to know he'd relay her information. "Three vehicles. Military-grade Jeep in the lead, two trucks behind. Fifty caliber on the Jeep."

Her gaze was pinned onto the computer screen in front of her as satellite images sent her the intel she needed to keep the Deltas informed. Each of them had the stealth and skill to do their job to fulfill the mission, but the support team gave them the necessary intel and assistance to not only complete the mission but also to make it back alive. Sure, she loved serving her country, but she was no flag-waving-in-your-face, chest-pounding patriot. In fact, those people made her skin crawl. Especially the ones who laid claim to military service or glory deeds they'd never done. No, it was her team that crawled into the belly of the beast to do what

9

needed to be done, knowing there'd never be public acclaim or even acknowledgment. Those were the guys that she'd do anything for to make sure they were safe.

"Tango has moved behind the second building on the right. Five men alighted from the vehicles behind the Jeep. Two entered the back of the building, two around to the north, and one stayed near the Jeep."

Her gaze never wavered as she watched her team alter their exit route based on the information she provided to the radio controller. She forced her heart rate to steady as the team maneuvered to take out the threat. It didn't matter that she'd been doing this job for this team for four years. She still held her breath, knowing the mission could go FUBAR at any instant. Watching as they successfully annihilated the Tango, she focused her eyes on their position until they neared the bird that would carry them and the man they'd been sent in to extract away.

Upon hearing Baker's voice over the radio, indicating they were in the air, she finally breathed a sigh of relief. However, she wouldn't feel relieved until she could lay her eyes on them. The team had been together for a long time. Occasionally, one member would leave, and another one would join the group successfully. They were her brothers-in-arms. Her comrades. Her friends. Especially Leo.

From the moment she'd first laid eyes on him, something clicked inside. It wasn't just that he was good looking, built, muscular... hell, a lot of the Special Forces she'd met over the years were good looking, making other men pale in comparison. It wasn't just that he was tall. Many of the men were over six feet and towered over her. It wasn't just that he was confident, intelligent, accomplished, and bordering on cocky. Because they all were.

Something had captured her attention the moment she'd met him. His thick hair fell in dark brown waves that were only tamed when he cut it short. But when it grew out, her fingers itched to move through the curls. His eyes were brown, tinged with amber, and when he turned his intense gaze toward her, she was mesmerized. His nose was straight, unusual that it hadn't been broken during his years in the service. She tried not to focus on his lips, simply because she had no doubt that the man would be able to kiss a woman until she forgot her name.

But what captured her imagination the first time she met him was the dimple in the middle of his chin. In her imagination, she would trace his jaw with her lips, settling her tongue along the groove.

In reality, she used her finger just to annoy him. He'd grab her hand, attempt to intimidate her with a pretend glare, and she'd laugh—each and every time.

The military transport plane the support team was on waited at the closest airfield for the Deltas to arrive. She left her computer open but stood and stretched her back, lifting her arms over her head. Moving over to Roscoe, their support medic, she helped him prepare for the rescue, knowing the man would need medical care as they flew back to the States.

After what seemed too long, a familiar noise was heard as the team returned, silent as they had left. Her gaze shot over, scanning the entire group. It didn't matter that their radio contact indicated the team was all safe and accounted for. Until she laid eyes on them herself, she didn't breathe easy. And, as always, her gaze rested on Leo longer than the others. Not long enough that anyone would notice, but she gave up pretending he didn't mean something more to her a long time ago. She'd also given up pretending they could ever be anything more than best friends.

She wanted Leo in her life and wasn't about to fuck up that friendship by trying to bring a different angle to their relationship that could blow up in their faces.

As usual, his gaze sought hers as well, and he winked. She offered a chin lift, the oxygen moving in and out of her lungs a little easier, then turned back to Roscoe. The mission wasn't over until they returned home and delivered the package.

Two days later, she walked out of the kitchen of her small apartment, two beers in her hands, and stopped, taking in the scene. Leo was slumped down on the cushions of her sofa, feet on her coffee table, shoveling in sesame chicken from a box of Chinese takeout in his hand with his eyes on the TV. The tight, faded T-shirt stretched over his chest and biceps, his tattoos snaking down one arm. The same view had greeted her for years, and she never took it for granted. And as she took in all that met her gaze, her smile widened.

His eyes cut over to her, and he swallowed. Inclining his head toward her hand, he asked, "You going to keep standing there hanging onto the beer, or are you going to come over here and join me?"

An image of *joining* him raced through her mind but was quickly squashed. "Keep your pants on. I'm coming." A snort slipped out as she shook her head. "Although, I have a feeling the woman I saw sitting in your lap when we got back to base probably said, 'Take your pants *off*. I'm coming.'"

Leo barked out a laugh, then reached for the beer in her extended hand. "Nah. Just wasn't feeling it that night. I went home alone." Looking back down at his food as he deftly speared more chicken, he said, "So did you leave with that visiting frogman?"

She shrugged, sitting down next to him and stretching her legs out so her feet rested on his shins. They'd hosted a training with a team of Navy SEALs for the week and took them out to a bar last night. One had made it clear that he had his eye on her, and she'd debated for most of the evening whether she would take him up on his offer. Seeing Leo with the woman on his lap had made her decision easier at the time but not overly satisfying. "It was okay. At least he didn't leave me completely wanting, but it wasn't quite the fireworks he promised."

"They're all fuckin' talk."

"Yeah, well, I figure if a guy has to brag about it, he must be lacking in some way."

"Fuckin' A." He swallowed, then added, "I never promise a woman anything. Not more than a few hours, and certainly not that I'm gonna rock their world. Hell, if we both get off and have a good time doing it, I figure it's a win."

Natalie bumped him with her shoulder. "You're a real romantic, aren't you?"

"I don't have time for romance, Nat. You know that."

She sighed and nodded. "Yeah, I do. Although... sometimes... I wish..."

He shifted slightly so that his intense gaze was pinned on her face. "What? What do you wish for?"

A myriad of desires, wants, dreams, and wishes flashed through her mind in an instant. And while she shared almost everything with her best friend, she kept some things deep inside. Like how much she thought of him in a way that had nothing to do with coworkers, teammates, or friends. Pushing those thoughts to the side, she quickly threw out, "Sometimes I wish to work with people who don't burp, snort, fart, and scratch their balls all the time." Shrugging, she added, "But we don't always get what we want, do we?"

Throwing his head back, Leo laughed. "No, Nat, I guess we don't."

Hearing his laughter and reveling in all the beauty that was Leo, she smiled. Taking a healthy swig from her beer, she settled in to watch the game with the best man she'd ever known.

"Why the hell are you knocking?" Leo called out as he jogged toward his door. He already knew it was Natalie since she'd just sent a text telling him she was there. She had a key to his place and usually just walked in. Throwing open his front door, he spied her standing on his stoop but did a double take as his gaze raked over her from head to toe. Her hair was down, falling over her shoulders, the tresses softly blowing in the breeze. She wore a little makeup, giving her face a glow. Her black tank top was tucked into faded jeans that hugged her figure. And instead of boots, she wore sandals.

"You gonna stand there and stare or help?"

Jolting at her question, he realized her hands were full as she juggled a bouquet, a six-pack of beer, and a plastic baking container.

He leaned forward to assist and grunted, "Sorry. You look nice. You got a date later?"

Lowering her brow, she huffed. "No. I thought I'd just get fixed up today." She jerked her head toward the driveway. "I've got a cooler in my car with some more shit."

"You brought all this?" He eyed the bounty, taking the beer from her hands.

"I couldn't show up with your family here and not bring stuff. The flowers are for your mom. The beer for your dad. And if Oliver is here, then you and he can fight over the cupcakes—"

Already jealous that she looked more gorgeous than ever when his brother was visiting, he wasn't about to share her special cupcakes. "No way is he getting the—" The words died as he was shoved to the side when Oliver barrelled into the room.

"Nat! Damn, girl, did I hear you say cupcakes?" Oliver asked as he grabbed her around the waist and lifted her off the floor, forcing her to hold the bakery box and flowers out to the side to keep them from getting crushed.

"Fuck, bro. Get your hands off her," Leo groused.

Oliver turned toward him, his grin in place as he continued to dangle Natalie in the air. "What's the matter, jackass? Jealous? Anyway, she brought the cupcakes because I'm here."

"Watch the flowers! Put me down, you big—*oof.*" The air rushed out of her lungs as Oliver squeezed.

Leo stepped closer, his hand closing over his brother's as he tried to pull his arm down. "Oliver…" he warned.

"Boys! Stop fighting over her and act like the gentlemen I raised!"

Leo rolled his eyes toward his brother as their mother walked into the room, and Oliver immediately set Natalie's feet back to the floor. His cocky grin was still in place despite the chastisement.

Natalie glared at them before turning toward their mother with a smile and was immediately engulfed in a hug. "It's nice to see you again, Mrs. Parker."

"You, too, my dear. And you know to call me Susie."

"These were for you, but I'm afraid Oliver's exuberance has flattened them," she said, shaking her head as she offered the bouquet.

"Hey, I was just excited to see you," Oliver said, reaching for the bakery box and then finding his arm slapped by Leo.

Susie sent a fiery glare toward her youngest son but offered a speculative gaze toward Leo, which he tried but failed to ignore. His parents had come for a visit since Oliver was able to stop over, as well. His brother, only eighteen months younger than he, had joined the Army and now served as a Ranger stationed at Fort Benning. Since their father had just had a birthday, they managed to squeeze in a family celebration visit from everyone.

"Nat!"

The booming voice brought everyone's attention to his dad, who'd just walked into the room.

"Happy Birthday, Mr. Parker—"

"Please, none of that! Just Sam or I really will feel old." He hugged Natalie and then shot a glance toward his two sons before lifting a brow toward his wife. "These boys misbehaving?"

"Of course," Susie quipped, throwing a mother's look toward her sons even though they towered over her.

"Only over pretty girls and cupcakes. What else is new?" Oliver laughed, peering into the bakery boxes while winking toward Natalie.

Leo heaved a sigh, but his mom intervened by leading Natalie toward the back door, where they set up a picnic. "I heard her say something was in the car, so boys, go make yourself useful!"

Natalie laughed as she walked arm in arm with Susie through the kitchen, Sam trailing right behind.

"Come on, asshole," Leo said, moving through the front door. "You have to leave early, so I know you don't want to miss any of the food."

The two brothers walked to Natalie's old SUV and pulled out the ice chest and spied another large cake box. Peering inside, Oliver whistled. "Damn, that girl made Dad's birthday cake? Gorgeous, smart, can cook—"

"No, she can't cook worth a damn, but she can bake."

Oliver planted his hands on his hips. "Seriously, bro? You're going to quibble over the difference between cooking and baking. Shit, you can always order out, but biting into one of her treats? Fuck, why can't I have someone on my team like that?"

Leo straightened and mirrored his brother's stance with his hands on his hips. "Hell, the way you go through women, the last thing you need is to have a temptation under your nose because I doubt you'd manage to keep from getting kicked off your team!"

Oliver laughed and shook his head. "I can't believe you've fought the temptation."

Leo bit back the hasty retort, refusing to let Oliver get under his skin. *No way he'd understand what it means to have a friend like her. And no way would I fuck it up!*

The afternoon passed the way he knew it would with his family. Good food, good fun. And laughter as his mom delighted in telling Natalie embarrassing tales of him when he was little. From the twinkle in Nat's eyes as she grinned over at him, he knew he was in for a world of teasing now that she had more ammunition. *At least Mom had more embarrassing tales about Oliver.*

When it was time for his brother to leave, he watched as Oliver hugged Natalie, kissed her forehead, and then said, "Are you sure you won't run away with me, darlin'?"

Leo held back his grin as Natalie waggled her finger

in Oliver's face. "You'd never be able to handle me, Ollie-boy!"

Natalie stepped back and allowed his parents to have their moment with him. Leo watched the familiar scene. His mother always blinked away a few tears when she said goodbye to them. Considering the inherent danger in their jobs, it was inevitable that each hug had the possibility of being the last. Their dad hugged next, then moved away with his arm around Susie.

The three made their way back inside the house, leaving Leo and Oliver standing in the driveway. Another heartfelt hug ensued, finishing with hearty back slaps. Separating, they held each other's gazes for a moment before sharing a grin.

"Take care, bro," Leo said. Though he was confident in his brother's Ranger team and Oliver's abilities, he knew missions could go FUBAR at any moment.

"Back at you." The look in Oliver's eyes was proof that he was thinking the same thing. Then he glanced toward the house and grinned again. "You've got a fuckin' great *friend* in there, my man. But then you don't need me to tell you that."

He shook his head. "Nope. I know." He braced, waiting, but for once, Oliver didn't pursue his teasing or prodding.

"Catch you next time," Oliver said as he tossed up a wave and climbed inside his SUV.

Leo watched as he drove down the street before turning toward his house. After another hour, Natalie said goodbye to his parents, and he walked her outside as well.

"You okay?" she asked, peering up into his face.

He didn't have to ask what she meant. He sighed and nodded. "Yeah. Oliver's always been a risk-taker, even more so than most in our business. But he always comes out on top."

She reached up and touched his chin dimple, and for once, it felt more like a caress than a tease. "See you at work."

He stepped back and let her settle inside her vehicle. Rapping his knuckles on the top as she put it in reverse, he waved until she was out of sight. Walking back inside, he wasn't surprised to see his parents sitting at the kitchen table with cups of coffee in front of them and another slice of cake in front of his dad.

He poured a cup of coffee and sank into a chair to join them. They sat quietly for a moment. The only noise was his dad's fork scraping against the saucer, finally ending in Sam's sigh of contentment.

"Susie, that was a mighty fine birthday picnic, and Natalie's cake was a winner, also." Glancing toward Leo, he added, "She's quite a woman, Leo."

He looked up sharply, his gaze bouncing between both parents, finding them staring at him. Lifting his hands, he shook his head. "Come on, guys. We've had this discussion before. Yes, Natalie is great. She's more talented at what she does for the team than anyone, and I'm not sure the team would go out if she wasn't there. But that's all. We're teammates and friends. That's it."

Sam had been in the Army many years ago and nodded. "Understood, son."

Susie sighed. "Well, as a mom who wants her son to

be healthy and safe, I'm thrilled she is so adept at her job. And as a mom who wants her son to be happy, then I'm thrilled you have someone like her as your best friend."

He began to breathe a sigh of relief, but then she continued, and the air halted as it left his lungs.

"But as a mom who would like to see her son with a woman who can fulfill the role of mate and one day be the mother of my grandchildren, I can't think of anyone better than Natalie, and I wish you could see that, too!"

He shared a beleaguered look with his father, who hid his grin but remained quiet, and Leo finally let loose the sigh that had been building. It wasn't as though he'd never thought of Natalie in a way that wasn't platonic—*hell, I've been plagued with those thoughts over the years.* She fit seamlessly into his family, into his life, and into his very soul. *But...*

"Okay, Mom, I hear you. But honestly, having her as a friend is the best way to have her in my life now." *And the only way.* He drained his cup of coffee, then stood and walked over to the sink, missing the expression passing between his parents.

3

THREE YEARS AGO

Natalie grimaced but steeled her expression as she walked from the ladies' room back into the bar near the American Legion in Tennessee, where her father was entertaining his cronies. That was nothing new. But considering Leo had come along, she felt raw with each story her dad told.

She would have never come for this visit, but the AL had decided to have a ceremony for members who also had a son or daughter in the military. When she'd received one of his rare phone calls, she knew something was up. She'd wanted to beg off and lie about having to be on a mission, but Leo, sitting next to her on the sofa when the call came in, gave her a hard stare, and she'd agreed out of guilt. After hanging up, she proceeded to fuss and fume about the request and trip, hoping to transfer some of that guilt to Leo. She had been unsuccessful because he just sat and grinned.

While she'd met his family several times over the

years, he'd never met her dad. And that was fine by her. But now, after the simple ceremony where she stood next to him, listening to the AL president talk about the honor of family members serving, they had come to the bar, and her dad's true colors were showing.

"Sure wished I'd had me a son like you, boy," Tony Robinson said, setting his beer mug down and turning his intensity toward Leo. His hair was now thinner and steely gray, but he continued to cut it high and tight as he had for so many years. "Nat does okay. The Army managed to do something with her, but damn, if she'd been a boy, she could have served the way you do."

Leaning back in her chair, she kept her mouth shut, slipping into the hard turtle shell that kept his barbs from stinging. Arguing with him over the years had done nothing to soften him. *God knows Mom tried to no avail before deciding to bail on him... and me.*

Leo leaned forward, his forearms resting on the table, and his narrow-eyed gaze was pinned on her dad. "Mr. Robinson, you do realize how amazing Natalie is, right? She's integral to all of us. Without her, we wouldn't have made it back in one piece on a lot of missions. To demean what she does—"

Her hand shot over to his arm, feeling the tense muscles underneath her fingers. She'd wanted to convey that he could save his breath, but her mind jumped sideways at the feel of his warm skin over steely, corded muscles.

"Oh, no, no," Tony said, shaking his head. "I'm not putting her down. I'm damn proud of her for making the support team for you Deltas. But I'm just saying that she could get in the thick of things if she was a boy. That's all." He took a final swig of his beer, then looked around.

She knew he'd extended all the goodwill toward her that he could and was now looking for his drinking buddies to finish the evening with. And she was done as well. She'd smiled more than she'd felt like. Shaken hands with more people than she'd remembered. And the beer was sitting in her gut, wanting to protest the overdone chicken wings and greasy fries she'd eaten. "Okay, Dad, we need to leave. Got a five-hour drive to get back to base."

Tony planted his palms against the table and pushed himself to a stand. "Good to see you, girl," he said, accepting her hug with an awkward pat on the back. "Glad you could make it. Take care of yourself, you hear?"

Forcing her lips to curve upward, she nodded and stepped back to allow her dad to shake Leo's hand. Tony pumped it firmly, thanking Leo for also coming, not seeming to notice Leo's hard, tight-jawed, narrowed-eye expression.

She turned and darted through the crowd toward the door. She didn't need to look back to know Leo was following. She felt him. It was instinctive. Her whole body came to life when he was near.

Glad to move into the fresh mountain air in the parking lot, she gulped in a deep breath. She dragged her fingers through her hair, pulling it away from her face and lifting it off her neck as she tilted her head back to the afternoon sky. She closed her eyes and let the sunlight beam down as she pushed the cloying afternoon events from her mind.

The feel of Leo's long fingers curling around her neck had her release a long sigh. Dropping her hair, she twisted around to peer up at him. She didn't say anything, feeling the need to let him speak first. *Or maybe not speak at all.*

He pulled her gently forward until she face-planted against his chest and his arms enveloped her. She turned her head to allow her cheek to rest against his heartbeat and lifted her hands to encircle his trim waist. He kissed the top of her head, then rested his chin there. They stood for several minutes, and she reveled in the safest place she'd ever known... his arms.

Finally, she leaned back and said, "We need to hit the road."

He hesitated as though getting ready to speak, then nodded. "Come on, Nat. We'll stop for some decent barbecue on the way home."

Grinning, she agreed. "Thank God!" With his arm slung casually over her shoulders, they snaked through the parking lot to get to his SUV. He'd insisted on driving and claimed he needed the extra legroom in his vehicle. She'd accused him of just needing to be in charge.

Climbing inside and buckling, she leaned against the comfortable seat and sighed in relief that he'd been so insistent. *I should have known this trip to see Dad would exhaust me.*

Once on the road, she rolled her head to the side and stared at Leo's strong profile. The curve of his nose, the arc of his jaw, the curl of his hair. All long ago committed to memory. "Thank you," she blurted.

He glanced over, a smile gracing his face. "Anytime, anywhere, Nat. You know that."

"Yeah, I do."

More silent miles followed, and she relaxed deeper into the seat. Then he looked over and said, "I know you'd told me what he was like. What it was like growing up with him. I guess I just never really understood."

She swallowed past the lump that appeared in her throat and shrugged. "He was a Marine down to his very marrow. Didn't know how to turn it off when he came home. Mom took it for as many years as she could. I know in his own way, he's proud of me, but he can't shake the idea I should be more." A long sigh left her lungs. "Oh, well. That was my annual visit to check on him, and you being there made it a helluva lot better."

Leo turned to hold her gaze before looking back toward the road. "Then I'll come next year, too."

Her heart skipped a beat at the idea that he'd do something just to make her life a little bit easier. Reaching over, she placed her hand on his arm, and just like in the bar, she loved the feel of the warm skin over steely muscles. "You would?"

"Of course I would. Anything for you." Then almost as an afterthought, he added softly, "What are friends for?"

She squeezed his arm lightly, then pulled her hand back. His words were true. His words made sense. His words were comforting. Yet his words left a small longing deep inside.

4

TWO YEARS AGO

Leo climbed from the passenger side of the limousine, his tailored tux fitting his tall, muscular frame to perfection. With his eyes covered in sunglasses, protected from the glare of the lights, he scanned the crowd, hating the way the masses pressed against the ropes aligning the red carpet. Seeing no obvious threat, he turned sharply and opened the back door.

Reaching his hand toward the person inside, he caught the smile of Camilla Gannon, hearing her whispered thanks. Assisting her out of the limousine, he kept her hand in his until she was steady on her sky-high heels, then waited as her assistant had fluffed and straightened the designer gown Camilla wore. He glanced at the jewelry about her neck, knowing one of the exclusive Hollywood diamond jewelers had loaned her the bling for the night, and choked back a sigh. Camilla was not only America's sweetheart actress but she was also a genuinely nice woman, making his bodyguard duties pleasant. Except for nights like this, when a threat could come at any moment. But this was his job, one he was paid well to do.

Life had taken an unexpected turn, but he was a firm believer in the old adage about one door closing and another one opening. He'd met Carson Dyer on a special operation a couple of years ago, and the two men hit it off. Carson had decided to get out of the Special Forces and set up his own security business in California. Bodyguards were a dime a dozen in the area, but Carson had already built up a professional reputation and had extended an invitation for Leo to join his firm if he ever decided to get out of the service as well. Leo was flattered but had no plans to take his friend up on the offer.

But a bullet through the shoulder necessitated a change. While he'd healed quickly, he lost full range of motion. A Delta who couldn't carry his weight, or rather the weight of one of his team members if needed, wasn't able to fully do his job. Unwilling to become a paper pusher, he considered the idea of becoming an instructor for the special ops school.

While it seemed everyone had their own opinion about what he should do, it was Natalie's thoughts that he'd sought. And in typical form, she'd stared him straight in the eye with her hands plopped on her hips and asked, "What the fuck do *you* really want to do?"

"I hate like hell to leave the team," he'd admitted. "But Carson's offer is a good one. Exceptional money. Not the same wear and tear on my body. Jesus, even regular days off."

She'd nodded slowly, and something he couldn't decipher flashed through her eyes, which was odd because he thought he knew all her moods.

"Then it sounds like you know what you need to do. Although, I do get a kick out of the thought of you being a bodyguard to the stars."

"You've talked about getting out yourself," he'd reminded her. "If you weren't worried about what your old man would say, you should do it, too."

She'd thrown her hands out to the side. "My dad would piss himself if he thought I was getting out of the service." Sighing, she'd dropped his gaze as she looked to the side.

He'd remained quiet, knowing Natalie's former Marine Drill Instructor father had not only instructed countless young Marines during his career but had also *drilled* into her that she should go into the service, as well. His domineering pressure finally got to Natalie's mom, who left him the minute Natalie graduated from high school and joined the service. Her father had nearly burst his buttons with pride when she made the support team for ACE.

She'd finally turned her gaze back up to Leo and offered a smile that didn't reach her eyes. "It won't be the same without you. Not just on the missions, but... well, who the hell is going to help me keep everyone straight? Drink beer with me? Laugh at my jokes? Bet on me when I challenge someone else to a drinking game? Listen to my tales of woe about my lame-ass dates?"

A pain had hit his chest, and he could've sworn it was his heart.

"Are you ready, Leo?" Camilla asked.

Jerking back to the present, he inwardly cursed at his inopportune trip down memory lane. "Yes, ma'am." He stepped to the side, allowing her to proceed down the red carpet, his sharp gaze on the crowd as she gracefully walked along, waving and smiling toward the photographers. He was partnered with another one of Carson's bodyguards, and together they made sure no one crossed the rope partition, occasionally stepping closer to Camilla as they threw a menacing glare toward an overexcited fan trying to thrust their autograph book too close to her. Breathing a sigh of relief when they'd made it inside the building, he waited until she was escorted into the secure area, then stepped to the side where the other security men and women waited.

Carson had proven to be every bit the boss Leo could have wanted, but dealing with other employees that were less professional than Leo was already taking its toll. Carson had recently traveled to Maine on a trip to meet with another former Special Forces buddy. He hadn't confided what the trip was for, and Leo hoped that Carson wasn't going to ditch his security business and leave Leo hanging. While ruminating on his future, his phone vibrated in his pocket, and he slid it out, checking the message from Nat.

Know you're at work. Got a glimpse of you on TV. You probably think your shit doesn't stink anymore, but remember I know the real you. Call when it's convenient. Need to tell you something.

He shoved his phone back into his pocket and covered his smile behind a cough. Not surprisingly, he and Natalie stayed best friends although their beer-pizza-game nights were relegated to monthly visits instead of weekly. He'd fly to North Carolina when possible, and she'd make it to California when she had the chance. Occasionally, they'd have a mission near the same area and would grab a drink or dinner if their plans could coincide. She gave him hell whenever she caught sight of him bodyguarding at a public event Camilla had to attend, and he gave her hell for anything he could think of just to be a pain in her ass.

But the reality was that while time and distance had not diminished their friendship, he hated not seeing her almost every day the way they had for years. He missed her laughter, her wit, and her beautiful face.

Sighing, he was grateful when the gala was over and Camilla was safely escorted back to her secure home. Leo headed to his apartment, anxious to get out of his tux, shower, and throw on something comfortable before settling in for a post-midnight call to Natalie. Thirty minutes later, he reclined on his bed with his back against the pillows and headboard and his long legs stretched out in front of him. He glanced at the clock, and even though it was a little after one o'clock, he knew she'd be ready to talk whenever he called. That wasn't being cocky— it was just the way their friendship had worked for years. He'd do the same for her anytime.

Hitting number one on his speed dial, he was

surprised when it rang several times before she answered.

"Hey, Leo. Glad you called."

His body tightened at her tone. "What's wrong?"

After a second's hesitation, she said, "It's my dad. He had a massive heart attack."

"Fuck, Nat. I'm sorry. Are you still on base? What hospital is he at? I can—"

"No, you don't understand, Leo. He's dead." Her voice broke. "He was such a pain in my ass, but he died so quickly. I didn't even get to fuckin' say goodbye."

"Christ, I'm so sorry." His supportive parents were a blessing, one he tried not to take for granted. But Natalie? Having met her father made him even more appreciative of his family. But then, even her contentious relationship with her father had at least been steady. When her mother divorced her father, she'd relocated, and while she and Natalie talked occasionally, they were never close. As far as the family went, her father was really the only relationship she had. "Where are you?"

"I'm driving to Tennessee right now. I should be at his place in about two hours. Once there, I'll have to figure out what needs to be done. I talked to one of his American Legion buddies who said they would help with arrangements."

"I'll get a flight first thing in the morning and should be there by midafternoon at the latest."

She sighed heavily. "Leo, you don't have to—"

"Shut up."

He grinned as he heard her snort.

"I'm pretty sure you're not supposed to tell a grieving person to shut up," she quipped, sounding more like his Natalie.

"Yeah, well, get ready for me to say all kinds of shit while I talk to you as you drive."

"You don't need to talk to me for the next two hours!"

"I don't want you falling asleep at the wheel."

"Leo, you need to sleep if you're going to get up in a few hours and catch a flight."

"Shut up," he repeated, still grinning when she snorted again.

For the next two hours, they talked. She reminisced about her dad, sniffed through a few tears, and laughed over the good times she remembered. They talked about his bodyguard job, his concerns about what Carson was doing with the business, and where that would leave Leo if Carson ended his company. They caught up on the comings and goings of the old team members. And by the time she arrived at her dad's house, safe and sound, he was comforted with the knowledge that he was in her corner, just as she would be in his whenever he needed. Disconnecting their call, he double-checked the flight plans he'd made while they talked. Setting his alarm, he caught a few hours of sleep.

By the time he arrived in the town where her dad had settled once he retired, he was anxious to see her, wanting to ascertain that she really was okay. As he hurried up the walk, the front door was thrown open, and she stood on the porch. Her hair was pulled into a sloppy bun, nothing like her regulation style. Red-rimmed eyes with dark circles underneath. And Christ, just like every time he saw her, she was heart-stoppingly beautiful.

Her face contorted in a sob, and she leaped down the front steps, racing toward him. He stopped, opened his arms, and braced himself as she launched into his embrace. He'd never seen Natalie be demonstrative with anyone other than him, and like everything about their friendship, he took nothing for granted. Holding her for a moment, he slowly settled her feet back onto the sidewalk. With arms around each other, they stood for a long time, his chin resting on the top of her head and her body enveloped by his. It felt good. It felt right. His best friend was settled close to his heart.

"You've got that crinkle in your forehead. What are you thinking?"

Natalie, sitting cross-legged on the floor, jerked her head up, offering a sharp glare toward Leo. Suddenly aware that the aforementioned crinkle must have surely deepened, she huffed. "You should never tell a lady she has a wrinkle."

"I didn't say a wrinkle. I said you had a crinkle."

"What the fuck is the difference?" she bit back, lifting her brows in an effort to smooth out whatever wrinkle-crinkle he was staring at.

"You're evading."

At those two simple words, which were admittedly true, she slumped her shoulders. "You know me too well." Her complaint wasn't true. In fact, it was because he knew her so well that she'd made it through the past five days.

She'd been amazed at how much she'd had to take care of, then scoffed. *Hell, I can handle logistics for a special ops team, but handling an unexpected funeral? Jesus, it nearly did me in.* She had no problem admitting that while she could've managed everything by herself, having Leo around made the ponderous tasks so much easier.

He'd gone with her to the funeral home, talked to some of her father's friends at the American Legion, and helped to arrange the service, including the wake held at the local chapter of the AL. They'd gone through her father's papers, finding his life as orderly as one would expect from a former Marine Drill Instructor. They'd made all the phone calls, all the notifications, paid bills, and talked to a real estate agent and his attorney. They'd packed up the mementos she'd chosen to keep and arranged for the donation of furniture, clothing, and household goods, following her father's wishes. The house and his modest savings all went to her. The attorney and real estate agent would work in her absence for the dispensation of his belongings and complete the sale of his home.

One of the week's surprises came from the papers found neatly stacked in his nightstand. Printed copies of the emails she'd sent to him over the years while she was in the service. Not abundant by any means, but at least once a month, she'd written a short missive telling him the unclassified version of a mission or what she was doing. He'd rarely replied with more than a "take care" response, but at least she felt as though she was doing her part to stay in touch. It was sure as shit a lot more than the nonexistent relationship she had with her mother.

Leo had taken the email copies and scanned them before sending them to her so that she'd have them preserved. Somehow he knew just what to do and when to make her swirling emotions seem less overwhelming.

In going through the family pictures which she'd found in neat photo albums in a box in the back of a closet, she now sat in the middle of the floor, discovering pictures of her parents in their early years of marriage and when she was a baby. It wasn't until the later years that her mother appeared to be forcing a smile for the camera. And while her father's smile had also seemed easier in the early years, by the time Natalie was a pre-teen, his face always bore the stoic or pissed-off expression of a drill instructor.

Looking up at Leo again, she shrugged as her hand waved over the album. "I'm staring at the photographs and wondering about the changes. Mom and Dad looked happy back then. And I guess I'm trying to remember what it was like. Or what changed."

"Tell me about your mom."

She pressed her lips together, uncertainty filling her. She'd spent so many years pretending her mom wasn't a part of her life that it seemed wrong to open old wounds. But Leo was patient as always, and before she knew it, she opened her mouth, and the words flowed.

"Mom used to hum when she'd clean the house and

make dinner. That's probably my earliest memory of her. Dad would come home, and they'd dance in the kitchen. I must have been only about four at the time." Glancing back down at the pictures, she added, "I see these old photographs, and Mom seemed really happy back then."

Natalie shifted so that her back rested against the chair, and she could face Leo fully as she talked. "I remember being in elementary school—probably first or second grade—and Dad was gone for a tour overseas for a year. And looking back, I think that's when the change started. When he came home, he was… harder. Less patient. More picky. He wanted my toys always put away and Mom to keep the house a certain way. He went through training to become a drill instructor, and we moved again. By the time I was ten, I knew Mom wasn't happy. She never smiled. She never danced in the kitchen. And when Dad got home at the end of the day, it was as though life was sucked out of the house."

Looking back down at the album, she noted, "There are very few pictures of us by the time I became a teenager. And God knows, those years were hard. Mom had sort of checked out. Present but not really there. She was tired of Dad treating us like his recruits, so she just retreated inside herself. I survived by getting his attention— first rebelling and then deciding to follow in his footsteps." A grin slipped across her lips. "Of course, I joined the Army and not the Marines. I thought he was going to have a fit!"

Leo laughed. "You had the ultimate rebellion then, didn't you?"

She nodded, still smiling. As the mirth passed, she thought back to her mom. "I suppose Mom felt betrayed when I joined the service. Looking back, she had already planned to leave when I graduated from high school, but in truth, she'd emotionally checked out years before. Dad was never abusive, just harsh. But Mom could have shielded me from some of that or at least explained it to my pre-teen self. My adolescent years of typical self-absorption didn't allow me to really see her loneliness. Instead, I just felt her withdrawal and then ultimately leave. She didn't come to my boot-camp graduation, but Dad did. She didn't celebrate when I made ACE support, but Dad did. So in a weird, fucked-up way, she left because the hard-ass Dad became didn't suit what she needed in a spouse, yet he was the only one who remained a somewhat involved, though pain-in-the-ass parent. But now, maybe I see that she did what she had to do to survive the only way she knew how."

Shaking her head, she closed the photo album, her nose tingling and her eyes beginning to prickle with gathering tears. "Christ, no wonder I'm a mess."

"Come here," Leo ordered.

It was on the tip of her tongue to toss out a refusal to his softly spoken request, but one look at the expression of understanding, not pity, on his face, and she shoved the album off her lap and took to her feet. He lifted one arm, and as she sat next to him on the sofa, he pulled her close. With her head resting on his shoulder, she breathed easier as they sat for long moments in peaceful silence.

Finally, he spoke, his words surprising her. "Your mom is still alive."

Leaning back so she could see his face, she asked, "You think I need to talk to her more?"

"I'm not saying you should do anything that doesn't feel right to you. If your birthday and Christmas call to her continues to be what you want to do, then keep doing just that. On the other hand, with your dad now gone and your perspective opening up, you can consider that maybe the future, while colored by the past, doesn't have to be written in stone just yet. She'll never be the mom you wished she had been all those years ago, but perhaps there is something new for the two of you."

They were silent again as his words moved over her. She closed her eyes and snuggled into his embrace even deeper. And she realized the emotion coursing through her wasn't so much about her dad or her mom, but about this man who cared enough to listen, advise, hold, and love her unconditionally. Dragging in a deep breath, she knew she loved him. More than just friends, but if that was all she could ever have, she'd take it.

At the end of the week, Natalie stood on the front porch of her father's house, still waving goodbye as Leo's rental car drove down the street on his way back to the airport. She stayed long after his car was no longer in sight, already missing his presence.

She was exhausted, yet she and Leo had spent each evening piled up on her dad's sofa with his legs stretched out so that his feet rested on the coffee table and her feet rested on him. Drinking beer. Eating take-out. Talking about everything and nothing.

Sighing, she walked back into her dad's house. She looked around and knew that if Leo hadn't helped, she'd have so much more that needed to be taken care of before she drove back to Fort Bragg.

Fort Bragg. For the first time in the ten years that she'd been in the Army, she truly questioned if going back was what she wanted to do. Her gaze moved around the space. Her father had not only given the military his career but also his life. To the detriment of his marriage. And honestly, to the detriment of the relationship he had with his daughter. She lifted a hand and rubbed her brow. *Oh, Dad, you chose your life, and while I've enjoyed my career, it's not what I want to do forever. I don't want to die alone with nothing but a few war veterans as friends.*

The idea of getting out of the service and following in Leo's footsteps had begun looming larger. One night after he'd gone to bed in the guest room, she'd spent time on the internet and discovered that female body-guards were in demand. She knew her stature was diminutive, but she also knew her skills. She could easily handle the job and would have the element of surprise on her side if anyone underestimated her abilities.

Moving through the house, she grabbed a beer from the refrigerator and settled onto a barstool at the kitchen counter. Alone for the first time in a week, she wished Leo was still with her. She admired his ability to adapt to what life had thrown at him. Wondering if she had that same quality, she turned the bottle up and took a large swig. *This is probably not the right time to try to make a major life decision or change.* But with her father's death, she knew change was already upon her. And after another swig, she smiled, hoping she was brave enough to go for it. *With Leo's blessing and him in my corner, maybe it's time.*

5

ONE YEAR AGO

Leo sat with several coworkers at a bar, enjoying a night off from the work that consumed most of their time round the clock.

Carson returned from Maine after meeting with another former Special Forces teammate, who'd created a highly specialized team within his investigation business. Mace Hanover started Lighthouse Security and Investigation, and his former special ops employees were known as Keepers, based on the old lighthouse keepers. Mace and Carson were now partners, and Carson created Lighthouse Security and Investigation West Coast.

Carson sold his security-to-the-stars business for a huge profit, as well as got rid of many of his former employees who were more interested in acting careers. Wanting employees that had also been involved in military special operations, Carson had asked Leo to join his new business. Leo considered himself fortunate to now be known as a Keeper.

Carson had purchased a decommissioned lighthouse on the coast, one that was small and not seen from the closest road. It was tucked into the hillside overlooking the water. Seventy-five acres of undeveloped land adjoined, mostly part of national forests. It afforded privacy, a place to train, and with the house and compound built into the hillside, the security was tight.

Although he knew the business would become as successful as the LSI in Maine, which Leo had visited, he also knew that it took time to build the facility Carson had in mind. So far, he'd been impressed with the speed in which Carson managed to get things up and running, but it took a lot of prep work before they could actually take on more complex cases.

Currently, they were mostly advising and setting up security systems more complex than what the typical security company could provide. They assisted with several investigations, gaining the expertise of Jeb Torres, a former SEAL who was a computer guru before completing the BUD/s course.

Carson had two administrative employees, both indispensable. Theodore Bearski, a sixty-three-year-old former sniper who'd never married and had been looking for something to do in his retirement. Teddy was now LSI-WC's weapons and equipment manager as well as a caretaker, looking after the acres of training grounds.

Rachel Moore was another bonus that Carson had hired. In her late fifties, the former Naval Intelligence officer was their administrative manager. She was widowed with two adult children, both in the Navy.

Like Teddy, she was looking to fill her retirement with something more than sitting around with her military memories and waiting for grandchildren.

Rounding out the Keepers was Hop, call sign for Frank Hopkins, their pilot, experienced in the field as a former Air Force special operator. Adam Calvin was a former Ranger. Frederick Poole, a former SEAL. Terrance Bennett, a former Ranger sniper. And Jonathan Dolby, Army Special Forces like Carson.

One of Mace's newest hires, Rick Rankin, decided to come to California to help Carson get things started. Rick's brother still worked for Mace, but Rick had decided he'd like to live on the West Coast. Easygoing and fun to be around, Leo already considered him a good friend.

And speaking of good friends, he looked at the dance floor as Natalie threw her head back and laughed with her current dance partner. Her hair was longer, now hanging to almost the middle of her back. Dressed in her typical black, it wasn't to disappear into the crowd tonight. *Not with every fucking eye in the place on her.* Her T-shirt wasn't skintight but tucked into her dark jeans and managed to show off every curve. She'd even given up her shit-kicker boots for cowboy boots for the evening. Swiping his hand over his face, he tried not to glare at the man she was dancing with yet knew if that man's hands dropped to her ass, all bets were off. *Wonder how Carson feels about his employees getting into a bar brawl?* Leo had a feeling that if it was to throw down for a lady's honor, Carson wouldn't mind. He winced. *Christ, Carson might not care, but Nat would have my balls for thinking she couldn't handle herself.*

She'd decided to get out of the service after her father died, but it took a while. She'd wanted to stay long enough to see the team through several upcoming missions plus train her successor. And she'd wanted to stay long enough to have her father's small estate settled and banked the money received. When she finally separated from the Army, the timing sucked... he knew Carson would have hired her for his bodyguard business if he was still running that.

But she needed a job and found one with another company. He'd checked into her new boss—privately, of course. Nat would have his balls if she knew he was going behind her back to make sure she wasn't working for some slime. What he found didn't make him happy, but only because he thought the guy was a money-grubbing prick. *But thank God, she's here in California.* She could have relocated anywhere but chose to be close enough so they could see each other whenever they wanted. And he had no problem admitting he'd be happy to see her every weekend. He rubbed his hand over his chest, a strange twinge moving through him.

Tonight, they were celebrating her new job and being on the payroll long enough to earn her first paycheck. She'd tried to say the drinks were on her, but he'd slipped the server his card, telling her that he was paying but to pretend that Natalie was. He also knew that Natalie would have his balls when she discovered that little subterfuge, as well. But the server winked, gave him her number, and told him what time she got off work. He wouldn't take her up on her offer tonight, even if Natalie hadn't been visiting. This bar was becoming the Keepers' place to hang, and he didn't want to face a one-night stand every time he walked through the doors.

"Natalie's amazing," Poole said.

His words dragged Leo's attention back to the other Keepers sitting at the table. "Yeah, she is."

"And you're not…?"

The question from Bennett hung out there, and Leo noted everyone's attention riveted to him. He hesitated, not sure how to answer. Oh, he knew what Bennett meant, but the fast denial that they were romantically involved no longer slid easily from his lips. He respected his fellow Keepers, but the idea of giving the green light to any of them didn't sit well with him. And the reason for that wasn't something he wanted to ponder. He took a sip of beer and then adopted a casual shrug as honesty was the only answer he could give. "We're not a couple. But she's the best person I've ever known."

"Then my next question would be, why not?" Bennett added. "Hell, man. Don't think you're going to find anyone better from a phone number on a napkin."

He flipped Bennett off to the laughter of the others. Nodding toward the napkin on the table, he agreed. "You're right about that."

"Hey, what's everyone laughing about?" Natalie said, returning to the table alone. She bent and picked up Leo's beer and took a long swig.

Before anyone had a chance to give him more shit

about her, Leo quipped, "Your dancing. Sure you don't have two left feet?"

She lowered the beer and threw a mock glare his way. "Everyone's a critic. Your dancing isn't any better."

"Why don't you prove her wrong?" Poole said, catching a wink from Bennett and a scowl from Leo.

"Come on, big man," Natalie cooed. "Show little ole me how it's done."

Shoving his chair back, he couldn't help but laugh. Little did his new coworkers know how often he and Natalie had danced together over the years. He nodded to the others. "Watch and learn, men."

To the hoots coming from behind, he grabbed her hand, and they linked fingers as they made their way to the dance floor. He gave her a twirl, then settled her to his side as an upbeat country song came on. Side by side, they executed a line dance they'd often enjoyed. It didn't matter that he was over a foot taller than her; their movements matched perfectly.

Now, with her head thrown back in laughter, he felt lighter than when she had been dancing with someone else. Grabbing her arm, he gave her a twirl just as the music changed to a slow song. She easily let him guide her in, and he held her close. Laughing and talking as they swayed back and forth, he knew they looked like a couple. Hell, one look at the expression on the server's face, and it was easy to see that she realized the number she'd left on the napkin would never get used.

Focusing his attention back on the woman in his arms, he traced the already-memorized nuances of her beautiful face. "Glad you came to celebrate your new job with me, Nat."

"Hell, Leo. I'm just glad to have a paycheck to celebrate with." She tilted her head to the side, her lips curving. "By the way, I know you gave the server your card instead of letting me pay for the drinks."

His brows snapped down. "How the hell did you figure that out?"

"Come on… I'm the best intel analyzer you've ever worked with, right?"

"Christ, you should come work for Carson. We could use you as we get into more and more investigations."

She sighed heavily. "Well, for now, I'll give the bodyguard business my best shot. Who knows? I just might have found my new calling."

She settled her cheek against his chest, right over his heart, and he bent to touch his lips to the top of her head. Familiar… and so fuckin' right, it scared him.

6

PRESENT DAY

Leo carried his loaded plate from the food-laden table and walked over to one of the picnic tables on the deck overlooking the ocean waves crashing against the rocks. The impromptu party was just what he and his coworkers needed after a difficult mission. Washing down the barbecue chicken wings and side dishes with cold beer, he enjoyed the lively banter and camaraderie. Leaning back, he looked around, appreciating his good luck. A great boss and coworkers who rivaled his Delta team in skill and camaraderie.

They were already able to handle most job offers coming their way. No more bodyguard jobs unless it was a special request, usually from the government. Contracts were offered through the FBI and other agencies. And the ability to choose which contract offers they wanted to take.

And on top of that, he'd had the pleasure of watching Carson fall and fall hard for a woman involved in their last major mission after his boss had protested that he didn't have time for a relationship. Leo had managed to talk some sense into his boss, and now, Carson's fiancée, Jeannie, joined them and tended to jump in to help whenever needed.

"Damn, this food is good," Bennett said, leaning back in his chair and patting his stomach.

Hop nodded, grinning as he licked the barbecue sauce from his fingers. "Hey, Jeannie. Where did you get these wings?"

The pretty blonde looked over from the other table and smiled. "Teddy and Rachel told me about Bobby's Barbecue. It's that new place in town. They're good, aren't they?"

"Damn straight," Poole agreed.

Rick shoved back his empty plate and looked toward Leo. "Did you finish that security evaluation this morning?"

"Yeah. The client has top security in his office building but is convinced he needs to keep most of his important work at home. I worked with the security installer and came up with what should be impenetrable."

Rick grinned. "And probably fuckin' expensive, right?"

Leo shrugged. "Hell, that CEO has money to burn. I tried to hold back, but he kept insisting he wanted more and more." The group continued to discuss several upcoming or accomplished missions. Finishing his plate, Leo stood and grabbed his empty beer bottle, walking over to the trash and recycle receptacles.

As the sun set over the water, he sucked in a deep

breath of fresh air, once again appreciating the view as well as his friends and employment. As he stood to the side, he felt his phone vibrate in his pocket. Pulling it out, he grinned at the caller ID. "Hey, Nat."

"God, save me, please."

Laughing, he shook his head. "Bodyguarding divas not to your liking anymore?"

"Are you serious? Hell, I never liked this job. Maybe if I had worked for Carson when he had his bodyguard business, I might have been happier. Or maybe if I worked with you, I might not be losing my fuckin' mind. Christ, I'd go back to the Army just to be a grunt if I could!"

"It can't be all that bad. Who are you with now?"

"Carlotta Caruso," she responded in a high-pitched singsong tone.

Leo barked out a laugh. "I know that can't be her real name."

"Who the fuck knows what anyone's name is here in Tinseltown? Hell, I'm not sure who I am half the time!" She must have heard the sound of laughter from those around him. "Oh fuck, I can tell you're at a party. Now I'm seriously jealous!"

"Just a work party. Time to kick back, eat, drink, and enjoy life," Leo said, suddenly wishing Natalie was with him.

"Yep, totally jealous. I've just been to a party to keep Carlotta safe from absolutely no one. Same old, same old. But she likes having someone around, so I was the one in a suit, standing in the corner, not drinking, keeping a watch over those prima donnas, divas, entitled pricks—"

"We've got to get together soon," Leo interrupted, hating that his closest friend was so miserable. "We'll catch up and talk seriously about getting you out of that job."

"It pays the bills," Nat quipped.

"Yeah, but you could have your bills paid and be happy," he insisted.

"Maybe. Anyway, I'll let you get back to your slice of happiness. Just called because I was bored out of my skull and wanted to make sure you didn't forget about me."

"Hell, we talk all the time, so I hardly think I'll forget about you. But carve out a time our schedules allow, and we'll meet at a bar and throw back a few."

"I'll hold you to that," she replied. "Okay, I've got to go. Believe it or not, I've got a real date. Dinner. Drinks. Maybe even decent conversation."

For a second, his chest squeezed like it always did when she was going out on a date with someone. Clearing his throat, he forced out a laugh. "No shit? You go, girl. Knock his socks off."

"If I'm lucky, I'll like him enough that I could knock more than his socks off! Talk to you soon, Leo."

"Bye, Natalie." Disconnecting, he slid his phone back into his pocket, her call leaving a smile on his face. He was still grinning when he rejoined the party.

Rick looked up. "Nat still hating life?"

Most of the Keepers had met Natalie since she'd hit a few bars with them after becoming a civilian. Like the other Deltas and support team, they found her hilarious and treated her like one of the boys. He'd been surprised when none had asked her out, but Rick explained that anyone with half a brain cell could tell that what she and Leo had should lead to more than just being best buds. Leo had snorted and replied that their friendship was special, and because it was so important to him, he wasn't about to fuck it up.

"Not so much hating life but hating her job." She'd quickly discovered that providing security for divas with a boss who cared more about the bottom line than his employees sucked.

"I know I've said it before, but for the life of me, I can't understand why you and she don't go for it. One of these days, you're going to wake up with regret."

He swung his gaze back to Rick. "Regret?"

Rick nodded. "Yeah. Some guy is gonna snatch her up, rock her world, and won't want you to be her best friend anymore. You'll find yourself on the outs and then realize you should've gone for it all along."

Leo opened his mouth to refute Rick's statement, but the idea that Nat would no longer be his best friend due to someone else's jealousy sat like a rock in his gut.

As the LSI-WC party broke up, several Keepers decided to head to one of the local watering holes to continue their drinking and see who they might pick up for the night. Leo wavered for just a moment, then shook his head as he waved them off. Bars and bimbos had gotten old, and as much as he loved his *bro-time*, he missed Natalie's quick wit when they were out.

Walking over to Jeannie, he bent and kissed her

MARYANN JORDAN

cheek, thanking her for the food and hospitality. With a
chin lift toward Carson, he headed around to his SUV,
ready to head home by himself.

Natalie sat at the table for two in a quiet corner of the
quaint restaurant. She'd taken extra care with her
makeup, and her hair fell down her back in waves.
Wearing a little black dress that still managed to be
modest, she wiggled her toes to relieve the twinge from
cramming her feet into too-high heels. She was even
wearing a lacy push-up bra, although she hated the way
it pushed her boobs up so high. But the extra effort had
been worth it based on the expression of appreciation
her date had offered as soon as she'd stepped through
the restaurant door. She'd insisted on meeting him
there, not wanting to be stuck if she needed a quick
escape, but she was pleasantly surprised at how well
things were going.

She lifted her glass and took a sip of wine, staring at
the handsome man sitting across from her. His hair was
neat but didn't look as though he'd spent a lot of time
prepping in front of a mirror. His suit accentuated his
broad shoulders, but she was glad he'd ditched the
jacket and gave her a chance to appreciate his arms and
torso with his fitted dress shirt.

He was a financial broker, a career that had the
potential to bore her to tears, but he said very little
about his job, admitting that he preferred to get to

know her more. A man who didn't constantly talk about himself was a welcome change.

When mentioning her military service, she obviously left off anything to do with the Deltas, simply saying that she'd been an analyst for the Army. When he'd asked about who she now provided security for, she'd stiffened, ready for him to begin gushing over the celebrities or angling for an autograph from one of them. When he didn't, she finally began to relax as the conversation flowed.

Just as she carefully sliced off a piece of her steak dinner, he inclined his head toward her plate. "You know, you really have to be careful with red meat. You never know where the beef comes from."

She blinked slowly as her fork halted in midair, surprised by his statement, which wasn't said with a condescending air yet sounded judgmental. Glancing down at his vegetarian lasagna, she lifted her brows while adopting a lighthearted tone. "Well, I might not know where it comes from, but I certainly know where it's going." With that, she slid her lips around the perfectly seared steak and enjoyed each bite. *God, Leo would love this meat.* When in the service together, they often searched for restaurants with the best steaks, vying for which cuts of meat had the most flavor. Jerking slightly, she pushed thoughts of Leo down, wishing she didn't compare every man to him and find them lacking.

"So what kind of music do you like, Natalie?"

"I'm eclectic in my tastes," she admitted. "I can listen

to jazz as easily as country. Heavy metal as easily as classical."

He smiled, his gaze pinned on her. "Hmm, that's a very generic answer. It sounds good but doesn't really give any information, does it?"

Once again, she stared, uncertain if he was trying to be condescending or simply socially awkward in trying to get to know her. Dabbing at her lips, she said, "It's not meant to be generic. I think music can be a reflection of our moods. I'm more likely to listen to heavy metal when I'm working on my vehicle. Country is what I want to listen to when I'm driving down a backroad. Classical helps keep me from wanting to murder people when I'm stuck in god-awful LA traffic on the highway."

Laughing heartily, he nodded. "I see what you mean. And I have to admit, I'm impressed that you work on your own vehicle. You're very accomplished."

She pinched her lips together, sucking in a deep breath before letting it out. "I confess I'm not sure if you're trying to get to know me or are purposely trying to tweak me."

His eyes widened, and he threw his hands up in supplication. "No, no, I'd never want to tweak you. I just want to get to know you better, and you are a constant surprise, which is good."

The server came around to whisk their plates away and deliver their desserts and coffee. Gliding her fork through the creamy cheesecake while making sure to scoop up some of the raspberry sauce on the bite, she closed her eyes as the sweet flavors hit her taste buds.

"Your cheesecake looks good," he said. Shaking his head, he added, "But I'm afraid it's not for me. All that dairy does something to my digestive system, and I'd have a stomachache for the rest of the night. Although some of the restaurant kitchen conditions might be part of the problem instead of just the dairy."

The idea of what the cheesecake would do to his *digestive system* completely knocked the pleasure of her dessert away from her. Laying down her fork, she watched as he devoured his peach tart and thought back to the last time she and Leo went through half a cheesecake where each slice was a different flavor, and they argued over the perfect combination. She'd have a bite and then let him eat off her fork, and he'd feed her some of what he'd tried. No worry about cheesecake and dairy. No worry about calories. And no worry about germs.

By the time the dinner was over, she was ready to go home— alone. She turned down his offer to go to a bar for after-dinner drinks and, fifteen minutes later, made a hasty escape after shaking his hand as they stood outside her vehicle. Closing her door with a resounding click, she started her engine and then watched as he climbed into his car and drove away.

Leaning forward, she dropped her head against the steering wheel. *I can really pick 'em!* While driving home, she thanked the dating gods that she had met him at the restaurant. As soon as she made it through her front door, she snapped the bolt and leaned against the wood, heaving a sigh. Toeing off her high heels, she walked to her kitchen and plopped her purse on top of the counter. "Jesus, what a fuckin' disaster of a date." *Granted, it wasn't my worst date. Not by a long shot. But still... when every man I go out with pales compared to Leo, I'm going to die an old maid because nobody's going to match up to my best friend.*

Checking her apartment's security, she stripped and took a shower, letting the hot water pound away at her tight muscles. Standing in front of the mirror as she dried, she plopped her fists on her hips. "Clear skin. Good muscle tone. Decent tits and my ass isn't bad. Can't help that I'm short. I'm fucking smart, and just because I won't put up with someone's bullshit, I should be able to get a decent date." *Yeah, but they're not Leo.*

Sighing, she padded into her room naked and dug through her drawers. Pulling on her sleep shorts and camisole, she grabbed her phone before climbing into bed. Typing quickly, she sent a text. **It's official. Men suck.**

It only took a few seconds before her phone rang, and she smirked. "Yes, it's true. Don't argue. Men suck."

Leo laughed. "Come on, Nat. Not all men."

"Fine, then just the ones I work for and the ones I date."

"Tell me all about it, girl. Get it off your chest, and you'll feel better."

Now it was her turn to laugh as she leaned back against the pillows, a contented sigh escaping. "Okay, first..." She regaled him with stories from the evening with her date, including his wondering where the beef came from, questioning her musical tastes, and learning about what dairy does to his system. Then they talked for the next hour, just like always, about anything and everything. And like so many times over the years, she wondered what it would be like to lay in bed together and talk. *Or do other things.*

Pushing that to the side, she relaxed as he made her feel better like he always did. By the time they disconnected and she slid completely under the covers, her heart was light as she relished their friendship. And she still wondered what it would be like to lay in his arms.

7

"Tad—"

"Natalie," her boss whined before he dropped his voice to a lower rumble. "The name is—"

"I know, I know. You want to go by Titus now. Jesus, why do you think a name change is going to matter to your business? I just don't get it."

"I've told you. In this business, perception is everything. Titus sounds tougher."

Natalie pressed her lips tightly together, knowing if she gave voice to the thoughts in her mind, she'd be out of a job. Thaddeus Jones. Her boss. A royal prick. His background included trying to get into the military but could never meet the weight or physical requirements. Took a few business classes at a community college, then met someone who said easy money could be found in the Los Angeles area as a bodyguard.

She had to hand it to him— he wasn't completely stupid. He'd gotten a loan, hired some former bouncers, and offered his services cheap to get his foot into the door of some agents. And considering plenty of people in the area wanted bodyguards, he managed to snag a few new but rising stars. Somewhere along the way, he decided that Thaddeus didn't sound like a tough enough name, so he'd recently announced that Titus was his new moniker. *Christ, shoot me now.*

When Natalie decided to take Leo's advice, Carson was changing his business and wasn't hiring. She'd met Tad— *Titus* just when he was expanding, and he loved the idea of a former military female as one of his employees. Not that he appreciated her skill set, but he figured she'd look good in his marketing campaign. *Fucking hell... stab me as well as shoot me.*

Of course, he didn't mind hiring a badass so he could promote that he hired her, but he didn't actually want anyone to act like a badass with him. She wasn't about to lick his boots for any reason, and her true nature always shone through. Hence the reason they'd butted heads, and he often gave her the worst of the divas to watch over. And Carlotta Caruso was about to take Natalie over the edge... or she was going to push the clueless actress over a nearby cliff.

"Okay, Titus. When you assigned me to Carlotta, you said it would be no more than a two-month assignment. It's been four months, and now you tell me that you've agreed for me to accompany her to Guatemala for a movie shoot? Seriously? Since when do you take on those kinds of contracts?"

As much as Titus continued to work on his image, he still couldn't keep the whine out of his voice. "Natalie, you know this would be a big deal. Carlotta likes you. She trusts you. Right now, she's got the studio eating out of her hands, and her agent called me and specifically said he wanted you there."

His eyes slid to the side, and her bullshit antenna leaped to attention. "Her agent? What the hell are you cooking up?"

Titus threw his hands up as he shook his head. "I'm not cooking up anything. You've got the looks that will show up great in their candid photo shoots of Carlotta on the set. You and Stan."

Her fists landed on her hips as her eyes narrowed. "Stan? Stan is going, too? You have got to be fuckin' kidding me! So that's what this is all about." He opened his mouth to speak, but she got there first. "That overblown, muscle-head hulk you hired as a bodyguard, even though he doesn't know the first thing about security but simply looks like a brick wall, has dreams of glory that someone's going to put him in a movie."

Seeing red, she turned and walked away, stalking to the window that overlooked the parking lot. Counting to calm down, she only made it to four. *Well, hell... that's not as far as the last time I had to deal with the boss, otherwise known as The Asshole.* Suddenly, clarity struck, and she whirled around, pinning him to the spot.

"Oh my God. Stan. He thinks that if he goes on this movie shoot to help guard Carlotta, he'll have a shot at a bit part. Christ, you're as delusional as he is to go along with this shit."

"Don't tell me how to run my business! But just for your information, even if he got a walk-on bit part or just got to know some of the other actors, he's agreed to push my company for more bodyguard jobs." He sneered, looking down at her. "You're sure as fuck not going to do anything to help me."

"Oh, really? I'm the one with the background who can actually do something if somebody was coming after Carlotta. Stan the Man wouldn't have the first idea what to do."

"I'm not arguing with you about this, Natalie. I've got my secretary making the arrangements for you and Stan to get down to Guatemala to accompany Ms. Caruso. You do the job that I hired you to do, and don't worry about him."

"You mean don't expect him to actually do any work, right? He'll be primping and preening, hoping to get on camera, and leaving the rest to me." She turned and stalked toward the door, the desire to tell him what to do with his job on the tip of her tongue. She'd met enough people in the business to know there were other job offers out there, but she grimaced and swallowed the words. It was too risky to quit a paycheck before having something else definite lined up. Stopping at the door, she looked over her shoulder, shaking her head. "You really are a piece of work, *Tad*." Without giving him a chance to reply, she moved through the doorway, barely resisting the urge to kick it with her booted foot. *Christ, I need a drink. I need to talk to Leo. Hell, I need to drink with Leo!*

Stomping toward Tad's secretary, who Natalie was certain had gone in for another boob job— *How many does that make? Three? And how is she even able to talk with her lips so poofed? I've heard of bee stung, but she looks like she ran her lips into a whole hive.* Deciding she couldn't be civil, she moved past the desk and called over her shoulder, "Just email my travel information to me," as she continued out the door.

She barely got out of the parking lot before her finger jabbed the button to place a call. The phone rang several times, and a stab of guilt hit her. *Shit, he's probably at work.* His phone connected, but just as she opened her mouth to begin her litany of complaints, Leo's oh-so-familiar voice came across.

You've reached me. Unavailable. Leave a message and your number.

A grin spread across her face at his very basic voicemail message. "It's me. Call me whenever."

She passed by one of her favorite bars, a small dive not frequented by the typical LA crowd, but figured she'd throat punch the first guy who tried to pick her up. *Okay... passing on.*

Pulling into the parking lot at her apartment complex, she glanced around, always conscious of security. It wasn't the best neighborhood, but it was affordable. At least it wasn't a total shit hole, for which she was glad. Once inside, she secured her door before heading to the kitchen to see what she might have for dinner. Standing with the refrigerator door open, she heaved a sigh. Beer. Wine. Cheese. Milk. Eggs. There were the makings for a salad, but that wouldn't cut it tonight. She liked to bake but hadn't had the time to go to the grocery store recently, so she didn't even have the ingredients to bake brownies.

Glancing at the clock, she decided it was a Chinese

delivery kind of night. But first, she had other plans. Stripping as soon as she got into her bedroom, she headed straight to the bathroom and started running the water in the tub. Throwing in a lavender bath bomb, she lit a few candles, climbed in, and sank under the fragrant water with her head against the back.

Showers were a necessity in the military and certainly great for expediency, but it was her little personal luxury to relax in a full, warm bath. In fact, now that she thought about it, Leo was the only person in the whole world who knew about her penchant for lavender bath bombs. He'd been over enough times that he'd sometimes jokingly complain that a game could make it to halftime before she would get out, and then he'd tease her about being a prune. She, of course, would threaten him with bodily harm if he ever told anyone since long baths would hurt her badass credibility.

Relaxing, she let her job, her boss, and her coworkers ease out of her mind. When the water finally cooled, she climbed from the tub and wrapped herself in a thick towel, another luxury she indulged in. Pulling on yoga pants and a worn, faded Go Army T-shirt, she walked barefoot back into her living room. After ordering her dinner to be delivered, she grabbed a beer and had just sat on her sofa when her phone rang. Grinning, she answered quickly. "It's about time you called me back!"

"Sorry! I was in the air and just got the message."

"Damn, are you on a mission?"

"Just landed in Alaska. Shouldn't be here more than a few days, though."

"Well, that sucks because, in a few days, I'll be in Guatemala."

There were a few seconds of silence before he repeated, "Guatemala? What the hell are you going to do in Guatemala?"

"Tad the Ass is sending me down for an entire month to babysit Carlotta Caruso on a movie set."

"Seriously? He's never done that before, has he?"

"No, and get this. He's sending one of the other meathead bodyguards just so that guy can hopefully get a bit part in the movie. I'm going because he can't trust Stan to do anything for Carlotta and thinks I'll also keep an eye on Stan. I'm so fuckin' mad, I'd quit this instant, but until I have another job lined up, that would be stupid."

"Shit, Nat, I've got to go. I'm sorry, but my security ride just showed up. Listen, don't do anything crazy. Stay safe and call as soon as you can. Once this job is over, you and I need to talk."

"Sure, sure, go save the damsel in distress from the bad guys." She tossed the phone onto her beat-up coffee table, wishing Leo's feet were propped on top. She really wanted to talk to him, both because he always made sense out of the crazy world and she knew he'd have her best interests at heart.

She finished her beer and had just gotten another when the doorbell rang. Tipping the deliverer, she sat back on the sofa and flipped channels, finally settling on another secret love, a baking show. *Well, a secret to everyone except Leo.* Watching as the chefs raced around making extravagant desserts, she shoved in sweet and sour shrimp, eggrolls, and crab rangoons washed down with beer.

Grabbing her laptop, she looked at the itinerary the human Barbie doll secretary had emailed. She had tomorrow to get ready, then flew out with Carlotta the day after. At least it was first class since the studio would be paying. Of course, that would be first class sitting next to Carlotta. *Or behind her. Oh God, there really is a hell.*

Leo accompanied Dr. Fredrick Carlsdale and his assistant out of the large lecture hall. The end of the conference signaled the soon-to-be end of this assignment in Alaska. It had been easy, but Leo never took any assignment for granted. Dr. Carlsdale was a world-renowned biowarfare expert, and the US government wanted him protected during this conference, hence the need for personal security outside the conference arena.

The scientist had been an interesting man to spend time with. He was brilliant yet able to converse on several subjects that had nothing to do with his career. Leo held open the door to the back of the SUV, his ever-vigilant gaze looking around as the doctor slid into the back seat. Climbing into the front seat next to the driver, he glanced in the back, smiling at the attractive woman sitting next to the doctor.

That had been another perk of the mission...

spending time with the doctor's assistant, Sherrie Mangus. They'd had the opportunity to sit next to each other at a few of the more informal meals, and while he never shirked his duty, he'd found her to be a down-to-earth conversationalist while at the same time having the educational background and experience to understand all of Dr. Carlsdale's research.

"Frederick, now that the conference is over, what did you think of today's sessions?" Sherrie asked.

"Excellent," he enthused. "I may have been the main lecturer, but I learned quite a bit from the others. I know you'll have the notes ready for me by the time we return home."

"Of course," she said with a smile. Her gaze shifted to the front as she said, "And now, the conference is over, and we can enjoy our last evening in Anchorage."

Leo didn't miss the not-so-subtle hint. Sherrie had shown an interest in him, but he'd been grateful that he had not needed to embarrass her by turning down an invitation. Having a relationship with a client... or client's employee could prove to be awkward at best, fatal at worst. Awkward if they had expectations that didn't meet his. Fatal if his level of diligence dropped due to the lack of attention. While Sherrie wasn't his assignment, her relationship with the mission definitely put her into a gray area. But the smile on her face directed toward him gave Leo the idea that with the conference over, there might not be the same conflict of interest.

"I'm having dinner at the hotel with several colleagues," Dr. Carlsdale said. "With the governor in attendance as well as other dignitaries, the FBI will provide any necessary security. Perhaps the two of you would like to have dinner at the same restaurant, but without feeling the need to stay right with me."

"That sounds lovely," Sherrie said, her smile widening.

An hour later, Leo shifted his gaze from the table where Dr. Carlsdale was enjoying his dinner, satisfied with the level of security, and focused on his own dinner companion. Sherrie's pale-blonde hair glistened in the candlelight, her blue eyes sparkling. She'd appeared for dinner in a pale-blue silk dress that flared over her hips, hanging to her knees. She'd greeted him warmly in the lobby as they walked toward the restaurant, his hand resting lightly on the small of her back. Now, drinks delivered and dinner ordered, they chatted.

"I can't tell you how nice it has been to have someone to talk to who's not part of this scientific community," she said, taking a delicate sip of wine. "Sometimes I think scientific researchers forget there are other things to talk about."

"I think that's probably how it is with many careers," he said. "We often hang out with those in our same fields. Therefore, conversations can focus on what we're most comfortable discussing."

"Well, I find your security career fascinating, but I'd much rather get to know the real you beyond your job," she said, her tongue darting out to snag a drop of wine on her lips.

Leo relaxed as the food was served, and they enjoyed

their surf and turf dinner. He was aware of the appreciative and interested glances Sherrie received from some of the other men in the restaurant, but her attention was riveted on him. A strange disquiet moved through him, and he glanced again toward Dr. Carlsdale but perceived no threat. Shifting his gaze back to find Sherrie's assessing gaze, he mumbled, "I'm sorry. Force of habit as well as my job."

She reached over and placed her hand on his, squeezing gently. "You wouldn't be who you are, Leo, if you weren't concerned about Frederick."

Conversation flowed from music to movies to sports. He hadn't felt this comfortable with another woman on a date in a long time. She was beautiful, educated, eloquent, and laughed easily. By the time the meal was over, Dr. Carldale was also ready to head upstairs. Sherrie and he escorted the doctor to his room, and after making sure it was secure and confirming their flight arrangements for the next day, he bid him good night.

Leo's room was next to the doctor's, but he walked Sherrie to her door just down the hall. She turned and placed her hand on his chest, looking into his eyes. She was tall and, with her high heels, did not have far to look to hold his gaze. Stepping closer, she smiled. "I was trying to think of something coy to say, Leo, but nothing came to mind. So I'll just be straightforward. It's our last night, and I'd really like you to come in."

Her words didn't surprise him—after all, the interest and sexual tension had been building over the past several days of the conference, and dinner had certainly given evidence of how compatible they were. But the disquiet he'd felt earlier coursed through him again. The image of the dark-haired, dark-eyed, petite Natalie moved through his mind. He inwardly scoffed, knowing she would have told him he should take the beauty in front of him up on her offer.

The light dimmed in Sherrie's eyes as he hesitated. She tilted her head to the side, her deep perusal unnerving.

"I was trying to figure out if I got the wrong signal, Leo, but I don't think I did. I think you're interested. I think you're tempted. I think you understand that I'm offering just tonight, but I wouldn't mind seeing you again sometime when we're in California. But the look on your face tells me that something holds you back. And I have a feeling it's another woman."

He startled, blinking several times. "Sherrie, I'm not involved with another woman—"

"Maybe not in a committed relationship, but I'd wager there's a special woman in your life."

Shaking his head slowly, he wondered why he didn't just grab her hand and lead her through her door, straight to her bed. "Just a really good friend, but we're not involved like that… not romantically."

She sucked in a deep breath and sighed, her lips curving in a small, sad smile. "Maybe not. Maybe not yet. Maybe not ever. But Leo, dear, I think you're kidding yourself if you think whoever that lucky friend is, she's nearer and dearer to your heart than you're admitting." She patted his chest, then turned and moved into her room. Looking over her shoulder, she smiled.

"Lucky lady. I hope she knows what kind of friend she has in you."

"I'm the lucky one to have her in my life." The words slipped from him, the depth of feeling surprising. He watched as Sherrie nodded before whispering, "Good night," and closing the door. He hesitated for a few seconds, wondering what the hell he'd just turned down and why. But instead of being filled with regret, he imagined Natalie's gorgeous expression as she would burst into laughter and couldn't keep the smile from his face. Heading a few doors back to his room, he entered. After a shower and changing, he slid into bed.

He played their last conversation over in his mind and hated that she wouldn't be home when he got there the next day. *Guatemala. She's in fuckin' Guatemala for a month. Doing a fuckin' job she hates.* He couldn't wait to talk to her again but first wanted to talk to Carson. LSI-WC needed a female operator, and no one was better than Natalie. She'd have reservations about talking to Carson, worried that working too closely with Leo could affect their friendship. But he knew nothing would change that relationship, and he was determined to do what he could to make her life better. Grabbing his phone from the nightstand, he quickly dialed her number, getting her latest answering message.

If you're selling something, no. Just no. If you're calling to remind me of an appointment, fine. If you're not calling to make my life better, hang up now. If you're actually one of the very few people I care about, leave a message, and I'll call you back.

Barking out a laugh, he shook his head. "Christ,

you're funny as hell, girl. Anyway, I finished work and am heading back tomorrow. Can't believe you're now gone. Call when you can, and as soon as you get back, we've got a date for drinks and catching up. G'night, Nat."

Disconnecting, he lay down and thought over his evening, still uncertain why he turned down a great invitation to spend one night burning up the sheets with a gorgeous woman, refusing to think of the reason she surmised. Scrubbing his hand over his face, he also refused to think of drinks and catching up with Natalie as a *date*.

Rick's words came back to him... *Some guy is gonna snatch her up, rock her world, and will not want you being her best friend anymore. You'll find yourself on the outs and then realize you should've gone for it all along.*

Sighing, he rolled over and punched his pillow, now wondering if sleep would come.

8

Four hours and fifty-three minutes. That was how long the flight was between Los Angeles and Guatemala City. Four hours and fifty-three minutes of sitting behind Carlotta and next to Stan. *And I haven't killed anyone yet. I actually haven't had too many urges to do so. That must be a record!*

Stan had been late getting to the airport, but that only served to make less time that Natalie had to be around him. Considering that Carlotta was wearing a floppy hat and large glasses in an effort to appear incognito while grumbling that no one recognized her, they'd been able to make it to one of the *lower VIP* lounges. They weren't actually called that, but Natalie knew that Carlotta would need to be an Oscar-winning actress to receive full airport VIP treatment. Nonetheless, she was just glad to be in a lounge, considering it made her job easier to keep Carlotta away from trying to be noticed by the masses of people who just wanted to get to their flight and then complaining that no one noticed her.

She'd wondered if Stan would make the flight when he came rushing up as they were ready to board. Beard trimmed, hair styled, and wearing a shirt with the sleeves rolled up to show his muscular forearms, it was all she could do to keep from stabbing her eyes. She was wearing black pants, a white blouse, and her shit-kicker boots, knowing full well that no one would look twice at her, which was the purpose of staying in the background.

Natalie was grateful that Carlotta had been on her best behavior, toning down her newly honed diva behaviors. And Stan's nose was buried in a book, which also surprised Natalie. She'd never seen him read anything other than a menu. When he closed the book and laid it on the seat table, she glanced at the title—*A Beginner's Guide to Obtaining Roles in Television and Movies.*

A snort erupted, drawing Stan's attention, but she morphed into a cough as she patted her chest, mumbling her apologies. "Sorry, my drink must've gone down wrong."

After their meal, he returned to reading, and she burrowed under headphones again, almost surprised when the plane began to descend. Having no trouble at the Guatemala City airport, she was pleased to see the studio had arranged for large, air-conditioned SUV rentals to meet them and the others working on the movie who were on the same flight. Stan held the door, then stood and flexed his muscles as he casually looked around before climbing in next to the driver once

Carlotta was tucked into the back seat. Walking around the vehicle, Natalie slid in next to Carlotta.

The driver smiled as he pulled onto the road. "I am pleased to make you comfortable. You will arrive at Santa Catarina in three hours. I will take you to the Casa Palopo. There you will find amazing views of the lake and volcanoes, gardens and pools, and restaurants that will provide you with any type of food you desire."

Carlotta turned toward Natalie and held back a little squeal as she reached out and grabbed her arm, squeezing. "Can you believe this? I've never been out of California before, and now I'm here in Guatemala!"

Natalie sighed, offering Carlotta a slight nod. As they maneuvered out of the city, she could not help but think of the difference between her and the young actress sitting next to her. Natalie was ten years older but felt a hundred years more wise, worldly, and worn the fuck out. She rubbed her forehead. It wasn't that Carlotta was a bad person. But she was young and inexperienced, living and trying to make it in a town that ate up and spit out the young and inexperienced. Carlotta had managed to snag an agent who was cutthroat, ready to push Carlotta into bigger parts, knowing he had complete control over her. At least he'd warned the young actress about her safety while on location. His reasons were purely to protect his cash flow, but Natalie was glad, hoping she wouldn't have to worry about Carlotta running wild when not filming.

Looking out the window, she appreciated the scenery but never relaxed. When with Delta support, she'd been in many Central American countries but had never spent time in Guatemala. Unlike many travelers, she was not enamored by the tropical beauty all around, knowing the dangers of traveling in a country ruled by corrupt politics and law enforcement and drug gangs.

Finally, at the end of their drive, the SUV driver dropped them off at the reception for the beautiful resort. There was a cheaper hotel not far away where most of the studio staff and workers would stay, but since Carlotta had snagged a leading role, she was afforded a villa in the nicer resort. It accommodated not only Natalie but also a Guatemalan assistant assigned to take care of them during the month. Stan would share a room at the resort with several of the studio's security personnel.

The check-in procedures went quickly, and Natalie and Carlotta were shown to their villa. Carlotta squealed and danced around as Natalie made quick work of becoming familiar with their surroundings. Three spacious bedrooms, each with a private bathroom, overlooked the lake. A large shared room with a fireplace led to various patios and terraces and a modern kitchen. An exclusive heated infinity pool and hot tub were also part of the villa. *Jesus! How the hell Carlotta managed to land a leading movie role and get to spend a month in this resort, I'll never know!*

It was hard to be excited about staying in such luxurious accommodations, considering the open-air rooms and pools were a security nightmare. Making a quick call to Stan, she ordered him to come to their room. Surprised that he quickly acquiesced, she showed him the layout of the area, tamping down her irritation that he was more interested in the infinity pool and hot tub than Carlotta's security. With the realization that he truly was there for his own agenda and not Carlotta's security finally cemented in her mind, she was determined to handle things herself.

A knock on the door drew her attention as an attractive dark-haired young woman walked in and smiled at her.

"You must be Carlotta. I am Abril De la Cruz, your assistant."

Natalie shook her head. "No, I'm not Carlotta. I'm Natalie Robinson, her personal security."

Abril blinked in surprise, then both women turned as Carlotta walked into the room. Abril looked back and forth between them. "Oh, my goodness. You two look so much alike."

While Abril moved to introduce herself to Carlotta, it was Natalie's turn to blink in surprise. *Look alike?* They both had long, dark hair and dark eyes, but Natalie barely pushed five feet four inches, and Carlotta was easily five inches taller. Natalie had natural curves on her lithe figure while Carlotta was reed thin. But now, as she stared at Abril and Carlotta standing next to each other, she realized that all three of them shared the same dark hair and dark eyes. Trained to notice small differences, it struck Natalie that other people could easily confuse the three.

"Is that all right?"

Natalie jumped, realizing that Abril was looking at her. "I'm sorry. What did you ask?"

"I was telling Carlotta that I had been given a daily schedule by the studio and would be arranging wake-up times so that she could get to the lot for hair and makeup before each day's shoot. I know that you will be accompanying her, so I wondered if you would like me to wake you, as well?"

"Thank you, no. The same itinerary should have been sent to me, and I can certainly get myself up whenever necessary."

If she sounded brusque, Abril didn't seem to mind. Nodding, she continued to smile. "I'll arrange the meals that will take place here at the hotel and anything else that needs attending to. I know you have a job to do, Natalie, and I respect what you need. If there's anything you'd like me to do, please let me know."

Her shoulders relaxed slightly, and Natalie nodded. "I appreciate that." Looking around, she said, "I think we should each get settled into our rooms first. I know Carlotta has to be on the set tomorrow, so I'll suggest you order dinner for all of us tonight to eat here." Seeing Carlotta's brow furrowed, she threw her hand up to halt any arguing. "Until we have a better idea of the setup of the resort and what your schedule looks like, you need your rest."

That response seemed to mollify Carlotta, and she nodded. "I hope I have time to visit some of the fun places and stores while I'm here." Turning toward Abril, she asked, "Is there a mall nearby? Or maybe some designer stores?"

Abril's brows raised, and her gaze shot toward

Natalie. "Uh… well, the resort has some nice shops and—"

"Carlotta," Natalie said, shaking her head, "you're here to work, not shop and sightsee. Plus, you need to understand the country you are visiting. Your food bill will be more than what most Guatemalans make in a year. So be sensitive to the culture around you!"

Carlotta's brow furrowed, and she chewed on her lip as she sighed. "Oh, well. I just remembered one of my roommates got to visit Paris when she was working as a model, and she talked about the amazing designer stores that she shopped at."

"This ain't Paris, babe," Natalie quipped, stealing a glance toward the wide-eyed, open-mouthed Abril.

Carlotta shrugged. "Pity. But maybe if I do really well in this movie, my next role will take me somewhere fun." With that, she headed into the larger of the three rooms, and Natalie dropped her chin to her chest, staring at her shoes for a moment.

"I confess, that was unexpected," Abril said.

Lifting her head, Natalie stared at the young assistant, seeing intelligence in her eyes and relieved not to have a Spidey-tingling that the woman was not exactly what she purported to be. It was obvious that Abril snagging the job of working with the studio during the duration they were in her country was a huge bonus for her. The pay and working conditions would be wonderful. *But then, she gets to experience all that Carlotta is. Jesus, I hope she thinks it's worth it.*

"Please don't judge all Americans by some of the tourists you meet or by some of the studio *elite*. Carlotta is young, and the studio is throwing money and perks toward her, many of which I think are over her head. But you'll find most of the people working on the movie to be hard-working and down to earth."

Abril smiled and nodded. "Thank you for that. I really want to be successful at this job. Several movies are being made here each year, probably because it costs so little for the studios to do so. But to be assigned to one of the lead actors was huge for me. I just want to make sure I do everything right."

"If you can keep Carlotta on schedule and take care of our food, I think you'll be golden. I'm going to head to my room and unpack, and I'll meet you back out here for dinner."

If Abril's smile was anything to go by, Natalie had reassured the young woman, so she counted that as her good deed for the day. *God knows that more than one good deed per day is exhausting.* Walking into the bedroom next to Carlotta's, she looked at the king-sized mahogany bed, peeked into her private tiled bathroom, then stood at the window to admire the beautiful lake surrounded by jungle and volcanoes. She let out a sigh. *Maybe, just maybe, this assignment won't suck.*

By the time Natalie crawled into bed that night after reviewing the security measures with Abril for the first time and with Carlotta for the umpteenth-illionth time, having a delicious meal of roasted corn risotto with lemon chicken served to their room, going over the studio's schedule for the next day and week, and even indulging in a dip in the infinity pool and hot tub, she was ready to crash.

She'd seen a message from Leo earlier but wanted to listen to it in private. Now, she grinned as he called her funny as hell and sighed when she realized he was coming back to California as she left. The idea of a future date of drinks with her bestie sounded perfect.

9

By the time Leo got back to California a few days ago, Carson and Jeannie had flown to Maine to meet with the original LSI owner, Mace, and his wife, Sylvie. He knew Sylvie now worked for LSI as their office manager since Mace had protected her and her son on a mission years before. He also knew that one of the original Keepers, Drew, was now married to an LSI employee, former CIA operator, Babs. *So it can be done... coworkers in a relationship.* At that thought, he jerked slightly. *Hell, Nat and I aren't in a relationship. Not like that. Just friends.* Swiping his hand over his face as he sat at his computer station, he sighed. Casting a casual glance to the side, he was glad that his behavior hadn't captured the attention of any of the other Keepers working in the office today.

By the end of the day, he continued working after the others had left, relieved when Carson walked in. "Glad you're back safe, boss. Everything okay in Maine?"

Carson grinned and walked over, settling in one of the nearby chairs. "Good as always. However, it was too cold for me. Love to visit there, but Mace and his Keepers can have the cold of the Northeast. Give me sunny California any day."

"I hear you," he agreed. "Did Jeannie enjoy the trip?"

Nodding, Carson leaned back in his chair. "She really liked it. She and Sylvie hit it off great, and I think she enjoyed meeting a few of the other Keepers' wives." Chuckling, he said, "I've got to tell you that I think she's ready to start matchmaking here. She says it's time some of you all started hooking up with someone for longer than a night."

"Hell, sounds like she's going to take over my relationship 101 lessons." He laughed.

Carson looked around at the empty room before his gaze came back to Leo's. "Any reason you're here late? I read your report on Alaska. Sounds like everything went smoothly."

"Assignment was perfect. No problems. I've been back for a couple of days and just thought I'd hang around to get a chance to say hello."

Carson's penetrating gaze held his. "Spill it."

Leo lifted his brow, but Carson jumped in before he had a chance to refute anything. "Leo, we've known each other a long fuckin' time. I can tell when something is on your mind, so go for it."

He sighed before leaning forward in his chair, his forearms resting on his knees. "It's about Natalie."

Carson nodded slowly, a grin playing about his lips. "She finally thinking about applying to work with us?"

He dropped his chin for a moment, then lifted his eyes to hold his boss' gaze. "Not exactly. I know she'd be an asset to the company. But I'm not sure I can convince her. She fears that because she and I are close friends, the friendship would suffer if something went wrong at work."

Tilting his head to the side, Carson continued to hold his gaze. "Do you share that concern?"

"No, I don't. Hell, we were best friends while serving together in the Army. She's smart, tough, and Delta strong in a way that made her the best support team member I have ever worked with. And I don't say that because we're friends. She grew up tough. Had to with her old man. He was a Marine Drill Instructor who always wanted a son, but since Natalie was his only child, he treated her as one of his recruits. Her mom couldn't handle life with her dad, so she cut out, leaving Natalie as well. She values our friendship but no more than I do. I think the difference is that she's used to protecting herself. So much so that when it comes to being afraid of losing her friendship, she stays in a job she hates with an asshole of a boss taking assignments that don't use her abilities. She's in Guatemala right now for a month as the bodyguard of some barely legal diva as she makes a movie."

Carson shook his head, choking back a snort. "You're right. She has so much more potential than that." He leaned forward, his gaze intense as he mirrored Leo's posture with his forearms on his knees. "Leo, I've got no problem talking to her. If she's interested in a job with LSI-WC, I don't see why she and I couldn't work out a mutually acceptable situation. What I'd really like to know is when are you going to get your head out of your ass?"

Jerking, Leo's brows snapped together. "What the fuck are you talking about?"

"Don't insult my intelligence by pretending you don't know."

Leo heaved a sigh, shaking his head. "I've known Nat for a long time. Longer than I've known you. She's probably the finest woman I've ever met. Hell, that was sexist. She's one of the finest people I've ever met."

"You want to know what I think?"

Leo didn't even pretend to hold back his snort. "I have a feeling you're going to tell me whether I want to know or not."

Carson grinned. "Damn straight. I think for a long time when you were younger, it was easy to be friends with her because she just seemed like one of the boys. You could drink, laugh, have fun with her, then go off and fuck a one-and-done." Throwing his hands up, he added, "I'm not passing judgment. Hell, that described most of us back in the day. But eventually, that gets old, and we look for someone we can build a relationship with. You helped me realize I had room in my life for Jeannie. Now I'm wondering when you'll realize that most women don't hold a candle to Natalie?"

Pinching his lips together, he couldn't refute Carson's words. Reaching up to squeeze the back of his neck, he shook his head slowly. "I already know that. But I also know that if I give in to those feelings and she starts working here, it could really fuck everything up. I care more about her having a good place to work, doing what she loves and is good at, than giving in to what I'd like to happen."

Carson leaned back again, his brows lifted. "So you're saying that you're willing to put up with the possibility of unrequited feelings on a daily basis here at LSI-WC as long as she's in a good work situation?"

"Abso-fucking-lutely."

Carson stood and shook his head, grinning. "In the language of relationship 101, that is the definition of love." They walked out of the room together, then stood overlooking the waves crashing below. "When she gets back from Guatemala, have her call me. Or if she doesn't, I might just call her."

Leo grinned, then walked to his SUV. He had a feeling that Natalie would be mad as hell at him for instigating this move, but if she worked at LSI-WC, he'd rest easier knowing her life was better. Even if they'd never be more than friends and coworkers, he'd take whatever he could get from her. *But maybe... just maybe, we can have it all.* With that thought ringing in his mind, he drove home, counting down the days until she returned to California.

———

Natalie rose early, as was her habit each morning. She made sure to get up at least half an hour before Carlotta woke so that she had private time for a swim in the pool and a dip in the hot tub. Abril was awake as well but stayed in her room or the common area, seeming to know that this was Natalie's private time. Grateful the assistant had that intuition, Natalie was able to begin each day fresh. However, her mood could plummet quickly, depending on Carlotta's behavior.

"Why is this called an infinity pool? There's nothing wrong with it, is there?" Carlotta asked as she stumbled out of her room, her hand already out for the cup of coffee Abril was handing to her.

Natalie climbed from the pool and looked over at Carlotta, her brow knit. "What do you mean?"

"Well, our clinic at school was called an infinity," Carlotta replied, pushing her hair from her eyes.

Christ Almighty. "That was an infirmary, not an infinity."

"Huh," Carlotta huffed, walking past on her way to the pastries and fruit laid out on a tray. "Well, no matter what it's called, it's a nice pool."

Abril and Natalie shared a look, both barely hiding their grins. It appeared that Abril was finally getting used to Carlotta's quirk and personality, and Natalie had often begged her not to base her opinion of all Americans on Carlotta.

Sighing, Natalie turned to look out beyond the pool. She had to admit that the scenery was beautiful around Lake Atitlan. The huge lake was crystal blue, surrounded by jungles and volcanoes. And much larger than she originally thought, being over fifty square miles and surrounded by numerous villages and little towns, each with its own personality. Since the movie was filmed mostly near the water south of Santa Catarina with some excursions by helicopter to Volcan San Pedro, Natalie didn't find the security too difficult.

By the end of the first week, Stan had acquired a small walk-on, no-dialogue part, but he immediately changed from even pretending to be there to help with security for Carlotta to thinking they were now co-actors—an activity that Carlotta didn't discourage, considering he pandered to her, driving up her ego.

Natalie had tried talking to Tad but to no avail. "Just do your fucking job and keep an eye on Stan, as well," he'd said on their last phone call.

"Fuck that," she'd retorted. "I'm on Carlotta detail. Stan can take care of himself unless you want to pay me double." She'd hung up before he'd had a chance to respond with what she knew would be an asshole comment.

For the most part, her days involved riding with Carlotta to the film set, where she'd be in her trailer for hair, makeup, and costume. Then while she was on the set, Natalie could sit back and relax since the studio provided security while actively filming. It was during those hours that she got to know Abril.

The young Guatemalan woman was just a few years older than Carlotta but much more mature. Natalie found that she enjoyed spending time with Abril, giving her a respite from her diva duties.

"Abril, I heard you speak French to one of the crewmembers earlier. How many languages do you know?"

A shy smile and a blush slipped across Abril's face.

"I'm fluent in multiple dialects of Spanish, English, and French."

"Okay, now you've got my curiosity. What's your story?"

Abril's brows lowered, and she tilted her head. "My *story?*"

"Your background. Your family. I've seen very few educated women in the past week in Guatemala, so tell me how you managed to stay in school."

Abril tucked her long dark hair behind her ear and shrugged. "I owe it to my parents. Even though I was a girl, they were excited that I could read and write so easily."

Natalie offered an encouraging smile, hoping that Abril would continue to talk.

Acting on that encouragement, she did. "I was born into a farming family. Neither of my parents had stayed in school for very long, needing to work on the farm. Most females don't stay in school longer than about four years." She hesitated, then added, "Only about a third of women in my country are literate. It's getting better, but very slowly. I was still in school at the age of twelve, and my *story* would easily have been different if it hadn't been for a chance visit by an educator from UNESCO. That's the United Nations Educational, Scientific, and Cultural Organization. The UNESCO educator spent time with me and said I had potential." At that, Abril blushed again, her smile widening. "They talked to my parents about me staying in school. They sponsored me to attend a boarding school in Guatemala City."

"Wow, you're very brave to have done that."

Abril blinked, her head jerking slightly. "Brave?"

Leaning forward, Natalie held her gaze. "Yeah, brave. You left your home and family to go to a school where you probably didn't know anyone else."

"No, I didn't know anyone, but I was terrified, not brave."

"Being brave doesn't mean you're not scared. It's moving forward when you are terrified that makes you brave."

Abril held her gaze before offering a shy smile. "There were other girls there like me, so I quickly made friends."

"And that's where you learned the multiple languages."

"I did well in many subjects but discovered I loved languages, focusing on English and French."

"What kind of job did you want to have when you graduated?"

Abril rolled her eyes and shook her head. "I didn't dare dream of a particular job. We filled out applications at the school, and they were all sent to various government agencies and businesses. I would have taken the first thing that had been offered."

"So you couldn't choose?"

"Not at first. That would've seemed presumptuous. But once I work in a field for a while and gain experience, then I can look for a new job if I want. I was lucky to be offered a position as a translator with the Department of Tourism. It's a government job that pays well by Guatemalan standards, especially for a female. I've been doing it for the past five years. This is the third movie I've assisted with."

Leaning back, Natalie took a drink from her bottled water, appreciating Abril's history as well as her candor. "Well, you might say you were terrified, but I'm so impressed with your story. So to me, you're incredibly brave."

Those words had the desired effect as Abril let out a huge breath, and her smile widened. "You are so nice to say so. I really like my job. I recently got a raise and am able to send more money to my parents. I get to spend time with people from other countries, and even though I'll probably never leave Guatemala, I feel like I have a chance to see the world through the eyes of the tourists I get to assist."

Natalie grinned. "I've seen a lot of the world, but you're a lot nicer than I am, that's for sure. I think if I had to deal with entitled tourists all the time, I'd lose my mind."

Abril laughed softly, her hand covering her mouth.

Normally, Natalie didn't chat with people, hating small talk and the implied friendliness that was fake, but with Abril, she felt at ease until the tables were turned.

"So tell me your *story*," Abril encouraged.

Immediately sucking in a quick breath, Natalie couldn't stop the grimace that crossed her face.

"Oh, I'm sorry," Abril gushed. "That was foolish of me to ask—"

"No, it wasn't. If I wasn't willing to talk, then I shouldn't have asked you questions," Natalie admitted.

Looking over the crystal blue water of the lake from their perch above where the actors were working, she sighed. "There's really not much to tell. My father was in the military, and as an only child and not the boy he so desperately wanted, I joined the military, also. Whether it was to please him or defy him, I have no idea, but at least it seemed to give me validity in his eyes."

"And your mother? Did she approve?"

Swallowing, she shook her head. "My mom took off about that time. My dad was a hard man, and I think she'd had enough. I was no longer at home, so she moved on. My dad died a while back, so it's just me."

"Oh, I am sorry."

"Yeah, well, it is what it is."

Cocking her head to the side, Abril repeated, "It is what it is? I haven't heard that."

"It means... well, um... it just means that the situation has happened, and there's not really anything anyone can do to change it."

Abril nodded. "Oh, I see. You can't change your parents, so your family is just what it has become. Is that right?"

"You nailed it." Seeing Abril's surprise, she laughed. "Sorry... I mean, you understand."

"I think I'll learn a lot being around you," Abril said, laughing also.

"Oh God, I'm not sure that's a good thing."

Abril's eyes widened. "I think you are the brave one. You said you traveled the world, but it was hardly a vacation."

Snorting, Natalie shook her head. "No, it wasn't a vacation, that's for sure." She reflected, and her mind shot back to her military career and her Delta support team days. Her lips curved slightly, remembering.

"I think you have a fondness that you are thinking of." Biting her lip in apparent hesitation, Abril blurted, "I think maybe a man?"

"A man?" she choked. "What makes you think I'm thinking of a man?"

Abril sucked in her lips. "Oh, I'm sorry. That was foolish of me, wasn't it? An independent woman like you wouldn't need a man."

Natalie hated that Abril was embarrassed. "Look, if we're going to be spending a lot of time together while Carlotta is filming, we need to get past the awkward part of getting to know each other. So say what you want. Ask what you want. If either of us doesn't want to talk about it, then we just say pass. Okay?"

Abril's lips curved, and she nodded. "Okay."

Sighing, Natalie leaned back in her chair. "So to answer your question—no, I don't have a man. I had some good friends in the military. One who is still my best friend."

"You have a man as a best friend?"

Grinning at the young woman's incredulity, she nodded. "Yep. Best friend I could ever ask for."

"Is he ugly?"

She barked out a laugh, as the image of Leo's handsome face and gorgeous body filled her mind. "Um... no. He's definitely not ugly."

"Claimed by another woman?"

"No. No other woman has ever had his heart." As the words left her mouth, she felt relief over the fact that no one had claimed Leo. It was selfish, but she hated the idea of their friendship changing when someone else came along who would lay claim to his heart.

Sucking in her lips again, Abril's brows lowered. "I think it would be wonderful to be with a man who was such a good friend. I think he would make the best man to be with forever."

Natalie's quick answer died on her lips, her smile slipping. She looked back over the lake, an ache forming deep in her heart. *Yeah, the best man to be with forever.*

10

"You've got to be kidding me?" Leo barked out laughter as he drove down the road. It felt good to laugh, and the early morning call from Natalie was welcome.

He was on his way back to LSI-WC headquarters for a special meeting. Carson's newest hire, Chris Andrews, arrived in California to begin work but was already embroiled in a mission. The Keepers had to fly in to rescue him and the woman he was traveling with, an artist named Stella. So now, Leo was on his way to work to join the others in investigating who had broken into Stella's apartment. The Keepers took every mission seriously, especially when someone threatened one of their own, including the ones they cared for. Then they went all out for protection and a dose of vengeance. But while his mind was on the case, taking a call from Natalie always put him in a good mood.

"Carlotta was puking her guts out as soon as the helicopter lifted off the ground. Her face was still green when they had her in makeup. So when they have to travel to a different location, she has to be driven, which means I have to go with her. Thank God, today is the last day for the filming at the volcano."

"Maybe you can toss her in to appease the Mayan gods," he quipped.

"Hell, Leo, she'd have to be a virgin to be any kind of good sacrifice!"

He laughed again while loving the sound of her delight, as well. "It's good to hear you laugh, Nat. I know this trip has seemed to last forever."

"Well, it's had its ups and downs. Stan walks around flexing his muscles all day. His bit part was over two weeks ago, but he thinks an agent will pop out of nowhere to sign him to a major movie deal. Too bad the thick muscles in his neck have cut off all circulation to his brain."

Leo snorted, but she was on a roll.

"Carlotta can be nice, but she's such a ditz. I swear, sometimes I wonder how she has managed to get as far as she has in this business, but then I look at her plastic-enhanced body and understand. She's getting bored with no nightlife and wants to go into the town to the closest bar. So far, I've managed to keep her from running amuck."

"How's the hotel? Still good?"

"Hell, yeah. We're still in the same resort I told you about. I swim every morning. The food is good. And most of the time during the day, I just hang out at the set, somewhere out of the way, and talk to Abril. She's young but smart and nice to chat with."

"Look at you, being all sociable and shit," he joked. "I might get jealous if you get a new best friend."

"You are my *only* friend."

"Did you just quote *The Mummy* to me?"

"As many times as we've watched it, I'd think you'd know the answer to that question. But seriously, it has been nice to have someone to talk with. I admit the movie crew is also pretty cool. Otherwise, I would have lost my mind down here for a month."

"So when do you come back?"

"There are only four more days of filming, and then they want a few days to do re-takes on location if necessary. So we're scheduled to fly back in a week. But I found out that Carlotta was invited to fly with the director on his private plane, so yours truly will be flying back solo on a commercial flight."

"Well, text me the details, and I'll come down and meet you at the airport."

"Thanks, I'll take you up on that. Okay, I'll let you go. Talk to you soon."

"Take care. Can't wait to see you, Nat." As he disconnected, his words resonated deep inside. He missed her and grew more determined to have her work for Carson each day. Friends. Fellow Keepers. *And more?* Shaking his head, he parked outside the lighthouse but didn't alight from his SUV, his mind turning over their situation.

It's time. Time to stop denying that their friendship could develop into more. Time to stop searching for a woman who interested him as much as Natalie when he preferred her company.

The sound of voices came from one of the other vehicles, jolting him to the task at hand. Now? Time to get to work. And in a week? Time to get to Natalie. Smiling, he walked inside the building.

The inside of the casino wasn't a surprise as Natalie looked around, but only because she had checked out their website first. The principal filming had wrapped up, and a group from the movie crew had descended on one of the larger towns around the lake and found an excellent place for drinks, dancing, and gambling for those who liked the risk. Carlotta had been thrilled to get out on the town and was determined to drink every cocktail with an umbrella that the servers brought. Natalie was stuck guarding the rapidly-becoming-inebriated actress while giving Stan the stink eye for getting paid to be a bodyguard while doing nothing but getting drunk, flirting with the other actresses, and losing his paycheck at the blackjack tables.

Standing to the side with Abril, whose brow was creased as she looked around, Natalie said, "Go ahead and drink. I'll make sure you get back to the resort with Carlotta safe and sound."

Abril scrunched her nose and shook her head. "No, thank you. I don't really drink, other than a little wine at dinner." She lifted her hand, waving it to the side, indicating the space around them. "This makes me feel... nervous."

"Nervous?" Natalie's gaze shot around, seeing a

crowd of people dancing to the left, people lining the bar on the right, and heard the sounds of laughter, bottles clinking, music, and the constant clanging of slot machines. Toward the back were several tables near the bar, filled with much of the film crew. A set of stairs near a hall where the servers came and went appeared to be guarded by a large man who Natalie could tell was packing a weapon underneath his suit. She assumed the high-roller games were on the second floor. To be honest, she didn't care what went on up there, as long as it didn't involve Carlotta. While she hated guarding the actress, who was rapidly on the road to being drunk, disorderly, and probably puking later, Natalie didn't feel a threat.

"It reminds me of places I was warned about in Guatemala City. I never went to bars because they aren't safe," Abril whispered, looking down.

Natalie had been in bars and casinos all over the world. Some looked like dives and had the best drinks and food around. Others were more upscale, but she knew the money that truly flowed was from drug gangs or other illegal activities. The young, especially females, had to be careful not to get snatched up by traffickers. So Abril's concerns were valid, but Natalie wanted to know more. "Anything specific?"

The young woman's gaze jumped to hers, and she shook her head. "No. But we were constantly warned when I was at school."

"That's being smart, Abril." She turned to keep an eye on Carlotta and sighed. "If you want, I can scoop up Carlotta and get you two back to the resort."

"No, no. We'll be safer staying with our large group."

"I agree. So while we're here, let's go hang where Carlotta is—"

"Even if you have to be near Stan?"

Rolling her eyes, she nodded. "Yeah, even if I have to be around him as well." Patting Abril on the shoulder, she encouraged, "Come on. If I have to deal with them, I'm dragging you along with me."

An hour later, Natalie knew that if she'd been there as just one of the crew, she would have had a good time. Drinking, eating, and just relaxing because the end of the filming was near. But keeping an eye on Carlotta was her priority, and the young woman wasn't making it easy. Natalie had steered her back to the group on several occasions when she'd veer over to the tables where a group of young men was hanging out, their eyes pinned on the pretty actress.

The last time she walked over to take Carlotta by the arm, Abril accompanied her. One of the young men looked at all three dark-haired, dark-eyed women and grinned. "Are you sisters?"

"Estúpido!" Abril bit out, taking Carlotta's hand.

"Aw, they're just being cute," Carlotta said, grinning sloppily. She looked over at Natalie. "You know, if you wore something besides black, you'd be happier. I think you should have more color in your wardrobe."

Fuckin' hell. "Okay, okay," Natalie said. "I'm tired, and you've still got a set call tomorrow for extra filming. I'm going to grab some of the others so we can catch a cab back to the resort."

Expecting Carlotta to refuse or complain, she was

grateful when she first nodded and then slurred, "I gotta go pee first."

"Let's stick together." Natalie sighed to Abril as the three women walked to the hall at the end of the bar. Thankfully, Carlotta was still mobile, and as soon as she took care of her business, the three women headed back toward the main room. Passing a group of men, Carlotta stumbled and fell against a large, suited man. Rushing forward, she and Abril managed to keep Carlotta upright, each grabbing an arm. As they started walking, they supported the inebriated actress.

Suddenly, Natalie felt a hand on her ass and whirled around. Her gaze landed on the closest man. Black hair, neatly trimmed and slicked back. Heavy, black brows. Tall, with lean muscles. Dressed much nicer than the other men around. His lips turned up on one side, and a smirk marred his attractive face but allowed his gold incisor to glisten in the bright casino lights.

Lifting a brow, she pinned him with her glare. "Didn't anyone ever teach you manners? If you can't get a woman interested in you legitimately, I assure you that grabbing her ass isn't the way to do it." She watched as his smirk instantly dropped, and the muscle in his jaw ticked as his eyes narrowed.

"You have no idea who you are talking to," he said in a deep low voice.

Barely aware of Abril and Carlotta stopping at the end of the hall where their film group had gathered, she held the man's gaze. "Fair warning, whoever-the-hell-you-are. Touch me again or any of my friends, and you'll lose a few fingers." Hyperaware, she felt the man's body vibrating with tension, and his fingers twitch. Two men on either side started to push forward. Not giving them a chance to react and make the situation devolve further than it already had, she walked backward, keeping her eyes pinned on him until she reached the group.

Seeing Stan leaning against the wall nearby, she growled, "For once, do what you're paid to do. Keep an eye on Carlotta as we get outta here." Stunned that he did as she asked, she kept Carlotta and Abril in the middle of the group as they went outside and climbed onto their bus.

As Carlotta giggled, sprawled out on the seat in front of her, Natalie scrubbed her hand over her face.

"You shouldn't have done that!"

Turning to look at Abril, she cocked her head to the side. "Done what?"

"There's an unspoken rule around these places. Don't stare at anyone. Not the men. Don't hold their gaze. They... the ones who are in charge..." Abril pinched her lips together. "To stare is an insult. And dangerous."

Lifting her brow, she waited as Abril swallowed deeply.

"My cousin was killed when he witnessed a crime, and the police came around to question him. He gave them a description and two days later was murdered. This was something else that they told us when I was in school."

"I'm sorry that happened to your cousin," Natalie said, understanding the culture was very different here for a female. "I wasn't trying to provoke him, but neither am I going to let a man like that get away with what he did." Sighing, she hated the fear she saw in Abril's eyes. "Look, it's all over with, and we'll be back at the resort soon. Let's put him out of our minds and focus on us."

Abril looked over and shook her head. "I think we're going to have to deal with the drunken Carlotta."

"Won't be my first rodeo," Natalie muttered. Seeing Abril's confused expression, she explained, "It means that won't be the first time I've had to deal with that."

"That can't possibly be in your job description, can it?"

A snort erupted. "As far as my boss is concerned, my job description covers anything the client wants. Since I don't want her choking on her own vomit, it wouldn't be the first time I've taken care of her. But I'm glad she doesn't have a fuckin' toy dog because there's no way I'd carry it around for her!"

11

Finally, after four weeks and three days in Guatemala, it was time to go home. Natalie was almost joyful at the prospect of being in her own crappy apartment and in her own not-so-crappy bed. She and Abril had spent the previous day helping Carlotta pack after she exclaimed she couldn't fit everything into her suitcase even though she hadn't bought any souvenirs.

While packing wasn't in her job description any more than some of the other mundane tasks she'd had to do, if it meant getting Carlotta on the plane and no longer Natalie's responsibility, she would have done it by herself and joyfully. But, as with most things for the past weeks, Abril made the shared time better.

The studio provided multiple SUVs and drivers for the principal actors and their entourage, so Natalie and Abril accompanied Carlotta back to Guatemala City. Once at the airport, the driver drove first to the building where Carlotta would get onto the private plane. The actress turned and threw her arms around a stunned Natalie.

"I can't believe you won't be with me when I get back. Are you sure you can't stay with me as my bodyguard?"

When Natalie had mentioned to Carlotta a few weeks ago that she was no longer planning on staying with her, Carlotta didn't seem to give it a second thought. "Um... sorry, but I'm looking for another job." Natalie wasn't sure why she blurted out that tidbit since she hadn't made up her mind, but the words felt good being released. As the younger woman held her tightly, she patted Carlotta's back awkwardly, itching to push away from the embrace. Abril's hand covered her giggle, and Natalie sent a narrow-eyed glare toward the amused assistant.

Suddenly, Carlotta sniffed loudly, then leaned back and smiled. "Well, Stan did mention that he hoped to get assigned to me. It seems he's become quite devoted!"

Unable to hide the roll of her eyes, Natalie sighed. "Yes, I'm sure he'll be very devoted." She watched as Carlotta turned and, with a wave, jogged to the stairs leading to the private plane. Looking at Abril, she grinned. "Devoted until he finds the newest star to hook his career onto!"

Abril laughed, no longer hiding her smile. "She certainly changes allegiance quickly, doesn't she?"

The two women fell into step as they walked toward the airport's main terminal. "You have several hours before your plane leaves, but the driver might hold your luggage while we go have some coffee if you would like."

Natalie hated the idea of sitting in an airport and brightened at Abril's suggestion. "That would be great." Checking with the driver, he agreed easily, saying he had the whole day set aside for his airport trip. With her Carlotta-watching duties over, she felt freer than she had all month. He dropped them off at a street near the airport, promising to stay close by to be available when she was ready to leave. There were cafés and restaurants up and down the street, and the tantalizing scent of food caused her stomach to growl.

The streets were teeming with vehicles and pedestrians, but they made their way along the sidewalk until Abril pointed at a small café with a covered patio overlooking the road. "Guatemala City has many coffee shops. I've only been to this one once, but I remember they had wonderful polvorosas… um, little cookies. They also have a heartier breakfast."

"Since I'll be flying soon, I think I'll skip the eggs." She laughed. Entering, she spied a modern coffee shop and, once they had ordered, walked back to the open-air patio, offering a perfect view of the daily life flowing around them. She felt a prickle on the back of her neck, but with a sharp look around, she couldn't see anything suspicious. Dismissing the notion as nothing more than a professional habit, she sipped the delicious brew and ate from the shared plate of pastries that Abril had ordered, feeling the tension of the past few weeks slide away.

The hustle and bustle seemed to ease away now that

she no longer had to focus on Carlotta's safety. Her mind wandered to the flight or, rather, what would happen once the flight was over. *Leo said he'd meet me. Will he already be there?* Normally, she would just go to her place, throw clothes into the laundry, go to the grocery store, then call him. The last thought curved her lips. Glancing back toward Abril, she realized the young woman had been quiet for several minutes. "I'm sorry, I'm not very good company, am I?"

"I could tell you were thinking," Abril said, her voice soft. "I know you're anxious to get home, but I would be remiss if I didn't tell you how very nice it has been to work with you." Blushing, she added, "I think you have become my hero."

Amused by her words, Natalie was also touched. "I should be no one's hero. If anyone is due admiration, it's you. You've risen to heights not often achieved by one your age in a country that doesn't offer many opportunities to women. And for what it's worth, it's been very nice to work with you, too."

The smile on Abril's face widened. "Maybe someday you can come back as a visitor. Perhaps bring the man who is your best friend. You know, I hear the sunset from a Guatemalan beach is beautiful. Perhaps you and he could enjoy it together."

"Are you trying to play matchmaker?" She laughed as a blush moved over Abril's face. She took another sip of coffee but had to admit the idea took hold. Sure, she'd seen lots of sunsets with Leo but never as part of a romantic scene. Maybe… one day…

The sound of squealing tires and the popping sound

of a weapon being fired cut through her thoughts. Her gaze snapped to the side as she instinctively grabbed Abril and shoved her to the ground, her arms wrapped protectively over the other woman while searching for the cause of the sounds.

Screams were interspersed with the noise of people running, chairs scraping, and glass breaking as tables were overturned. The popping did not continue, and an eerie silence fell over the street.

Crawling over to the patio railing where the pedestrians had fled, disappearing like roaches in the daylight, her gaze landed on a man standing near a black SUV with tinted windows while clutching his chest, blood covering the front of his shirt. He dropped to his knees, staring toward the vehicle as a man in the passenger side held a weapon out the window. Natalie couldn't take her eyes off the scene, noting the killer glared before he climbed from the vehicle. Walking forward, he looked down at the bleeding man leaning to the side as he remained on his knees. Lifting his weapon, the assassin shot the man in the head before glancing around, his expression appearing to dare anyone to look. Turning, he walked back to the vehicle where the back-seat passenger had now rolled down his window to view the spectacle.

Furious, Natalie leaned forward with her hands gripping the rail, her gaze riveted on the black SUV, impotent to be able to do anything but stare. As the man in the back seat cast his gaze around the now-clear street, his gaze lifted to her as she remained in full sight on the patio with the sidewalks now deserted. *Him!* She recognized the man from the casino... the one who she'd threatened. Her heart pounded as the adrenaline coursed through her. Instinctively, she leaned forward, ready to leap over the rail, but her training had her halt. She had no weapon... no way to protect herself or anyone else.

"Natalie! No!" Abril cried out, pulling on her arm.

The man's gaze landed and stayed on hers. Then a slow smile curved his lips, his gold tooth glinting as his tinted window slowly rose, taking his smirking expression from her sight.

As the SUV sped away, tires squealing once again, she jerked from Abril's grip and raced out into the street, quickly memorizing the license plate. Looking down at the murdered man lying in a gruesome position, she grimaced at the sight, clenching her fists at her sides.

Abril rushed over, averting her eyes, and grabbed her arm again, pulling. "Come on, come on. We have to get out of here!"

"I recognized him... the man in the back seat," she bit out. "I also got the license plate—"

"No, you can't do anything about it! We've got to get out of here before the police come. If they have any idea that you could identify the man or that vehicle, they will come after you."

She remembered Abril's comments about the corrupt police and her cousin. Plus, she had enough experience around the world to know Abril was right. People were beginning to mill around, so she gave in to

Abril's pull on her arm as they hustled back down the street where they'd left their driver.

Shaking with rage, she glanced over to see Abril was also shaking but knew it was from fear. Wrapping her arm around the young woman's shoulders, she sucked in a breath and let it out slowly, reminding herself that she'd seen a lot of shit over the years all over the world. Abril might have been exposed to some of it, but she'd also been sheltered by her family, the Guatemalan school she'd attended, and now the job she'd obtained.

When Abril finally pulled back, she swiped her face and sighed. "Natalie, I'm so sorry."

"You've got nothing to be sorry for. I'm sorry that my actions back there scared you."

"You're brave and wanted to do what was right and natural to you. But me? All I could think of was running away, like everyone else."

Natalie ran through her options and knew she needed to get Abril out of the area. She grimaced. "Sometimes running away is the best thing you can do. As much as it rubs me the wrong way to let this go, you were right. Something about their actions was so blatant, almost as though they wanted to taunt me into doing something." She scrubbed her hand over her face and straightened her spine, placing both hands on Abril's shoulders. "As much as I hate for us to leave each other this way, right now, I know we need to say good-bye. You need to get to safety, back to where you live. I'll go to the airport and get through security. Once home, I can let someone know who might be able to get the information on the perpetrator to the right authorities. I want to know that you get home safely, so text or call me when you get there."

Abril agreed with a nod, her mouth pinched tight. "As much as I wanted to spend more time with you, I want to make sure you get to the airport safely. But again, I say, it's been an honor and a pleasure to get to know you."

"Hey, this isn't the end," Natalie said, gaining the other woman's intense gaze. "Believe me, it's rare that I find anyone I want to spend time with. Being with you for the past several weeks has helped keep my sanity. So call, text, email... whatever works for us to stay in touch."

Pulling each other in for a tight hug again, Natalie finally separated, then lifted her hand to signal for the driver who was still parked where they'd left him. Climbing inside, she leaned closer to the window and waved. The SUV pulled out onto the street. With her phone in her hand, she was ready to press the number for Leo. She planned to tell him what happened and get his and Carson's opinion of how she should handle the situation. If they told her to leave, she would. If they advised her to go to the police, she'd do that, too.

A scream erupted from behind them, and she jerked her head around, spying a man with his arms around Abril, lifting her off the ground. He backed up several steps then turned, still holding her in his arms. Another black SUV with dark tinted windows came to a stop, and the back door opened. Abril was struggling, but he handed her to a second man, and they transferred her to the back seat. The door closed, and they pulled onto the road going in the opposite direction after doing a u-turn, scattering more pedestrians.

The license plate was different, but everything about the SUV looked just like the first, and Natalie wondered if the smirking man was responsible. "Go!" she screamed to her driver, leaning over the front seat. Pointing toward the SUV that was disappearing, she shouted, "Follow! Seguir!"

"No!" The driver spoke in rapid-fire Spanish, and while Natalie couldn't understand him, she had no doubt he was telling her he wasn't about to put his life on the line. Throwing open the door, she leaped from the back seat while grabbing her phone. She snapped a picture of the back of the SUV as it moved farther down the road before running toward it. It turned the corner, and it was long gone when she made it to the intersection. Her body shook with fury and rage, and she almost missed the feel of her phone vibrating in her hand, indicating an incoming text.

Hey, Nat. Hope your flight goes well. See you when you get here.

Punching the speed dial, she didn't give him a chance to answer. "Leo! I need you!"

12

Leo's heart skipped a beat when he'd heard Natalie say she needed him in a way that he'd never heard before from her. She was always so calm, even in the middle of a fucked-up mission. But now, her panic resounded in her words and spurred him to race toward the LA airport parking lot, glad that he was close. He'd driven down early to meet her to avoid some of the worst LA traffic, planning to kill time until her arrival later that day. But as he'd listened to her sustained recitation of the events she'd just witnessed, all thoughts of fast-on-his-feet mission planning flew from his mind, and he was filled with one thought only—getting to her before she headed out to find her friend with no backup.

"You get somewhere public and stay there," he ordered. "Stay safe and don't move until I get there. I'm serious, Nat. Promise me." Those were his last words before disconnecting so that he could call Carson, knowing LSI-WC would not hesitate to jump in. Sure enough, giving Carson and the other Keepers in the office the sit-rep Natalie had relayed, he worked to steady his breathing as they made plans.

Carson immediately stated, "We'll get you to Guatemala faster than trying to arrange commercial flights." As the others asked questions, it only took a moment for Carson to return. "I've got Rachel making arrangements for a private plane leaving from LA. She'll send the details to you in a few minutes."

"Why the hell would someone grab a Guatemalan assistant?" Rick asked.

"I have no idea. All I know is that in the last month, Natalie has mentioned Abril several times as being smart, helpful, very capable, and someone Nat enjoyed talking to. Considering she's an excellent judge of character, I'd say we can assume that she had this young woman pegged correctly. But I don't know anything about her background or what Abril may have been involved in." He pinched the bridge of his nose, shaking his head slightly. "Shit, I don't even know her last name. Give me a second, and I'll text—"

"No worries," Jeb replied. "I've already pulled up her name from a security list from the movie set. Abril De la Cruz. Give me a second, and I'll get her information. Okay…she's university-educated and works for the Department of Tourism. Let me grab a photograph."

It was only a moment before Jeb spoke again, but Leo could've sworn time was crawling.

"I've got her picture. Sending it to you now, along with her records."

Dolby came on the line. "She's pretty. Dark hair and dark eyes. Kind of similar to Carlotta Caruso."

Rick jumped in. "Maybe the kidnappers got the wrong person."

Another Keeper, Bennett, added his thoughts. "Could be they saw someone with Natalie and thought it was Carlotta. Possible kidnapping for ransom?"

"Anything's possible," Leo said, scrubbing his hand over his face. "I know when I worked for Carson as a bodyguard to some Hollywood types, Carlotta was seen as an up-and-coming actress, but mainly because she'd stumbled into a couple of decent supporting roles. But not working in that world anymore, I sure as fuck don't keep up with who's who in that crowd. Natalie doesn't seem to think much of her, but that's more about Carlotta's personality and not her cash value in the business."

Rick re-entered the discussion. "Because I know Natalie, and I've seen Carlotta in a couple of movies, I can easily tell the difference. But at a quick glance, all three women have similar features with their dark hair, dark eyes, and builds. That would definitely support the idea that they meant to grab Carlotta instead. Hell, they could have grabbed Natalie, thinking she was Carlotta."

"If that's true, then Abril's life won't be worth anything when whoever grabbed her realizes they have the wrong woman," Carson said.

His boss had simply stated what had already hit Leo, along with the staggering possibility that they could have taken Natalie instead. *And I would never have known what happened to her.* That thought alone caused his footsteps to stagger as he hurried along the sidewalk. "Natalie will not stop trying to find her, that's for sure. I've told her to get somewhere safe and not to move until I get there." *And her life won't be worth anything, either, if she's caught along with Abril.* His stomach dropped, and he tried to push those thoughts from his mind, praying she followed his instructions. "Anything on my flight?" He knew his words were sharp but was beyond trying to hold on to his professionalism.

"Rachel is finishing up the arrangements now. Chris is working with Jeb to send everything we're pulling up to you. Hop is going to fly Rick down as soon as they can, so you'll have backup for whatever you need. Also, Dolby and Poole are on standby to get there if needed. Whatever you need from us, it's yours."

The weight on his chest lifted ever so slightly. "Thanks, boss... everyone. I'll head down as soon as I get the information from Rachel. Once I meet up with Natalie, I'll be in contact." Feeling relieved with a partial plan in place, he drove to the private airstrip of one of Carson's contacts, glad he had little traffic to contend with.

Parking outside the small hangar, he walked to the back of his SUV and pulled out the duffel he kept at the ready. Change of clothing, radio equipment, body armor, passport, secure laptop, and a few other items that could always come in handy. Securing his vehicle, he jogged toward the building, meeting the pilot that Carson had secured. Soon he was in the air on a private plane to Guatemala, his stomach in knots and his mind muddled, but knowing he would soon have Natalie in his arms, he focused on the situation.

The pilot glanced over, then leaned forward to change radio frequencies. Glancing toward Leo, he said, "Your boss is on the radio."

Nodding his thanks, Leo tapped audio for his headset.

"Okay, here's what we've discovered so far. Abril De la Cruz was born in the Huehuetenango area of Guatemala, known for its agriculture, including opium. There's not much on her family other than birth certificates and basic family records. Her parents are farmers, but they don't own their own land. They work for a large farm that grows corn, beans, and potatoes. But like most farms in the area, those can be covers for the opium that's also grown. Looks like there was a police record about her cousin, who was murdered several years ago. Male, twenty-one years old. He'd reported a crime to local police and was gunned down in the street. Abril snagged a boarding school position and left home, then attended university. Seems like someone noted her intelligence and gave her a path to a better future."

"But considering her family, there's the possibility that whoever snagged her meant to get her, and it wasn't a case of mistaken identity with Carlotta?" he mused aloud.

"There's no way to know right now," Carson admitted. "At this point, you have to assume that anything's possible."

"Can you get a message to have Natalie talk to us?"

Jeb asked. "There's not a lot you can do in the air, but if she can tell us more, that puts us further along in the investigation. We can call her through a secure channel."

"Yeah, hang on." He quickly typed out a text and hit send. **You'll get a call from my boss on a secure line. Talk to us. I'm in the air and will contact you as soon as I land.**

A few seconds later, his phone vibrated, and he looked down. **Working with the boys who have the cool toys. Be still my fluttering heart.**

Losing the battle to keep the grin off his face, he shook his head. "Okay, Carson, she's ready. Have Jeb patch the call to her and me so that I can listen, as well. Then as soon as I land, I'll get to where she is and be ready to go with a plan." After a few seconds and several clicking sounds, he heard Carson's voice.

"Natalie? This is Carson Dyer. I assume Leo let you know this is a secure line."

"Yes, I'm aware, and it's good to hear from you, Carson."

Leo, his chest squeezing at the sound of her voice, jumped in. "Nat, my ETA is about three hours, just to let you know."

"Are you safe, Natalie?" Carson asked.

"As far as I know, yes. I'm pissed as hell, upset as shit, and ready to kick some ass. But since I didn't know what the fuck I was up against, I checked into a small hotel using cash. It's not a complete dive, but neither did they ask for my passport or ID. It's probably one step up from a rent-a-room-by-the-hour, but since I have no intentions of sleeping on this bed that probably has more cooties than I care to think about, I'm fine. There was a street vendor just outside, so I bought some food and a cold beer. Hell, for me, this is a typical Friday night."

Jesus, Natalie. A chuckle erupted from more than just Leo, and he knew the other Keepers listening to the call shared his admiration of her.

"Glad to hear it, Natalie," Carson said, his usual voice giving in to her humor. "To bring you up to speed, we've looked at Abril De la Cruz. Her family. Her history. We know about her cousin's death after going to the local police. Her family works on a farm, and you're probably not surprised to learn that the farm may grow opium as well as other crops. But with what we can discern, her family is poor and probably simply tending whatever the farm owners tell them to grow."

"That's the same information she gave me, without the part about the opium. Whether she knows that or not, I have no idea. She left home years ago, and while she still visits her family, I doubt she's out where they work."

"Natalie, this is Jeb. What can you tell us about the man sitting in the back of the vehicle? The one you recognized from the casino."

"I need to make it clear that he wasn't at her kidnapping, and I can't figure out how they could be related, but the vehicles were similar. Both new, black, clean, tinted windows. A fuckuva lot more expensive than any other vehicles in the area."

"We understand, but Carson can get your information to the proper authorities."

"Christ, I had actually told Abril that I would do that, but that flew out of my mind after seeing her taken."

"I'm sure. But anything you can tell us, we'll pass along," Carson encouraged.

"If I say Hispanic, black hair, and dark eyes, I can already imagine you rolling your eyes. But beyond that, he was at least five feet eleven inches, maybe six feet, which made him taller than the other men around. His hair was trimmed... actually groomed like he had a barber on call twenty-four-seven. His face was clean-shaven. His clothing was expensive, tailor-made. He had a gold crown on his right incisor. Because he was wearing a suit, I wasn't able to see any tattoos or other markings, but he did have a gold signet ring on his right hand. A man's face. But I couldn't determine any writing."

"Narco saint," Jeb mumbled.

"What?" Natalie asked.

"Send her an image," Leo ordered.

"On it," Jeb agreed. "If you just described what I think you did, then it could be a Sinaloa cartel signet. If so, that's a huge tie-in."

Waiting for her to receive the image, they listened as Carson continued to ask more probing questions, not surprised at the amount of detail she was able to give. Make and model of vehicle. License plate. Description of the two men in the hall of the casino and the assassin that was in the vehicle.

"Yep, that's it," Natalie confirmed. "It was gaudy as hell, worn on his right ring finger."

"While anyone can purchase one of those rings, with

his description, I'd say he was someone with money and connections, along with the protection of the cartel," Carson surmised.

"Are you looking at the assassination and her kidnapping as part of the same group? The assassination could easily be tied into cartel wars, but Abril?"

"We don't know anything yet—" Leo began.

"So you think they grabbed Abril because of her family?" Natalie asked, her voice exposing her incredulity. "If for ransom, they'd get nothing from her. And if for trafficking, there were a ton of other females on the street that would have been just as easy, if not easier to grab."

"Nat," Leo called out calmly, knowing she was spun up and needing her to focus on the facts, which was always her strong suit. *Being personally involved in the crime has knocked objectivity right out of her.* "There's no way to know now about the assassination being tied into anything. But we've been bouncing around the idea that perhaps they didn't mean to grab Abril. Perhaps, they thought she was Carlotta because they are similar in appearance. Maybe they had seen her with you and thought she would be worth a ransom."

For several seconds, Natalie was quiet, and Leo knew she was already running various scenarios through her quick mind.

"I admit that I'd thought of that possibility. Not at first, because after spending a month with both women, I didn't think about their similarities. But if someone was in haste, didn't consider there could be someone else with me, they could have thought they were getting their hands on an American actress they could hold for ransom." She sighed. "Shit, this sucks not to be able to go after them. I ran down the street, but there was no way I could get close."

"Fuck, Nat—" Leo growled.

Carson jumped in, interrupting. "You don't want to hear this, but that's for the best, Natalie. Without a weapon, they could have easily taken you, as well. Then we'd have no witness, no way of knowing what happened, and no way of being able to help. If they were after Carlotta, they won't hurt Abril. They'll keep her somewhere safe, giving us a chance to get there and find her."

"I'll stay here for another couple of hours, Leo. Then I can catch a taxi to the airport."

"He's landing privately, not going to the airport. You stay where you are, Natalie," Carson demanded.

Jeb added, "I've got your location, and when Leo lands, I'll send him to you. In the meantime, I'm running your description of the man through all the databases I can, as well as the casino security cameras, and will start sending pictures for you to go through to see if you can identify this man."

She snorted. "Well, well, I guess I am playing with the big boys now."

Leo heard the others chuckle in the background, and he wasn't sure if he wanted to wring her neck or hug her. Probably both and at the same time. "I'll be there as soon as I can, Nat, and we'll work this together." As the words left his mouth, he knew he wanted to be with her a lot more than just this mission. And not as just best friends.

Sighing, he scrubbed his hand over his face. He just wasn't sure how to make it all work, but a slow smile curved his lips. *I'm damn well going to figure it out.*

13

Time seemed to crawl as she scanned through photographs Jeb sent to her while waiting for Leo's arrival. Each minute represented more time that the kidnappers had Abril, and that thought sent chills through Natalie. She hated feeling helpless and longed to jump into action but knew in her heart she had no idea where to begin.

While working as a Delta support team member, the missions were planned by others with little input from her. Once in place, she was an expert in the behind-the-scenes mission management, making sure Leo and the others had the logistics and intel to be successful. But figuring out how to find a kidnapped woman in another country? *I don't have the skills myself to do this.* And while she was smart enough to acknowledge that fact, it made her stomach churn with anger.

Anything yet?

Staring at the text from Jeb, her fingers jabbed at the keys. **If I'd recognize someone, you'd know about it.**

Now looking at her snark-infused message, she sighed before erasing it, typing another message, and sending it. **Not yet. Hopefully, something will hit.**

"They'd better appreciate how polite I'm trying to be," she grumbled to herself. Just when she thought she'd go mad, a knock on the door jolted her from the bed, her heart in her throat. With no security peephole, she placed her ear against the door and listened. A smile spread across her face as the light tapping of a secret message came through. Throwing open the door, she grinned up at Leo.

Just as tall as ever. Just as muscular as ever. The wave in his hair was just as familiar as the angles of his face. A tight T-shirt tucked into jeans did wonders as it pulled over his thighs, and she didn't need him to turn around for her to know the denim would also make his ass look drool-worthy. Forcing her gaze back to his face, which was no hardship, she watched as his eyes moved from the top of her head down to her toes and back. His gaze was both assessing and comforting. It had been over a month since she'd seen him, yet it felt like yesterday and years ago, all at the same time.

Without hesitation, she leaped forward, not surprised when his sure embrace encircled her, crushing her to him with her feet dangling in the air. The crazy world seemed more sane. The stress and anxiety felt less. The wrongs were righted. The rage was eased. And more than all the other emotions slamming into her was the feeling that she was right where she belonged. In his arms. With this man. Her best friend.

Refusing to give in to the tumultuous thoughts,

fearful of them showing on her face, she simply hugged him tighter, deciding to revel in the moment. And she was sure it wasn't her imagination that his arms held her even closer as his lips pressed against the top of her head.

After probably only a minute, she forced her head to lean back so she could stare into his eyes. She expected a wide grin, maybe a smirk, a twinkle in his eye, and surely a smart-ass comment about her hanging on him like a monkey. Instead, a muscle twitched in his tight jaw, and his expression held a mixture of concern and anger.

"Hey," she said, drawing his gaze to her eyes. "I'm okay. Maybe not great, but I'm okay and a fuck of a lot better now that you're here."

He opened his mouth as though to speak, then closed it, offering a curt nod instead. She thought he would set her down, but it appeared he was content to hold her above the floor. Now feeling a bit foolish, she wiggled. "You can probably let my feet touch the ground now."

"I could," he agreed, still holding her.

"Okay, I'll amend my statement. As glad as I am to see you, I feel goofy dangling in the air."

Finally, his lips quirked upward. "As short as you are, I would think you'd appreciate the extra few inches."

Snorting, she shook her head. "Don't mind saying that you're the best sight walking through my door, and after over a month separated from my best friend, I'm glad we're back together. But we've got work to do."

He sighed and nodded, lowering her to the floor.

"Agreed. But I also don't mind telling you that the idea of you being in danger didn't sit well with me at all. You and I've got a lot to talk about, but we'll have to wait until this is over." Leaning down, his face was directly in front of hers. "But we will talk, Nat, but just like you've indicated, I never want to be separated this long again."

Suddenly, the room felt small, like the oxygen had been sucked out. He appeared so serious that she had no idea what he meant by his words. And the situation didn't allow for them to try to figure it out at the moment. Swallowing deeply, she simply nodded. Looking back toward the edge of the bed where she had been sitting, she said, "I've been going through pictures of the cartel leaders but not coming up with anything. Jeb was just tapping into the casino security cameras, which he said weren't sophisticated but also weren't very organized, so he had trouble finding the one from the night I was there. You're just in time for me to start going through that."

"Got it, but not here. We're getting out of this dump and heading somewhere nicer that's closer to the casino." His gaze looked behind her, spying her luggage, and shook his head. "I know you travel light. Is that all you've got?"

She shot him a grin. "You know me very well. Yeah, that's it. This and my purse. The only thing I had out was my phone." She immediately shoved it into her purse before they turned and leaned forward at the same time, each grabbing a bag in perfect unison. With a quick glance around, she followed him out the door, not surprised to see an SUV outside. It wasn't tricked out like the one she knew he had with LSI-WC, but neither was it a rental. A few small dents and scratches and regular license plates. Tossing her bags in the back, she spied his duffel already there. Climbing into the passenger side, she buckled and then looked toward him. "Where did you get the wheels?"

"Carson had it waiting for me. Not a rental, so we'll blend in better."

"Smart thinking. But then, you were always brilliant."

"Hell, thank God for Carson and the other Keepers. Somehow, the idea that you might be in danger fried my brain!" He pulled out into traffic, pulling up the GPS coordinates on his phone.

"You said we were going to go somewhere closer to the casino, but that takes us east, back toward the resort I just came from."

"There's another resort Carson has for us that's only a mile away from the casino you were at. Pretty nice, but not as fancy as what you've been in." He glanced toward her and grinned. "Hope that's okay?"

"Gee, I don't know, Leo. I'm not sure if I can make it without an infinity pool and hot tub," she quipped.

He chuckled, shaking his head. Her phone vibrated, and she looked back down. "I'll start going through the security stills that Jeb is sending while you drive if that's okay?"

He nodded, and she slowly started moving through the multiple video angles from the night she'd visited the casino with the others. Occasionally, she looked up to see Leo deftly handling the vehicle along the roads and stealing glances at him as often as she could without being obvious. In the middle of a fucked-up situation, just having him with her made it easier to breathe. And harder to concentrate, considering that this was the first time she'd been in his presence after giving in to the desire to be more than just friends.

"GPS says it will take us about two hours to get there."

"That's fine," she said, jerking her gaze back to her phone. "It'll probably take me that long to review the security pictures." She settled back, comfortable that they'd make good time with Leo at the wheel, and the mission could now progress. Squeezing her eyes for a few seconds, thinking of how scared Abril must be. *Survive, girl... just keep surviving.*

After what seemed like interminable, eye-fatigue squinting, she jumped. "I've got him! Hell, I've even got where Carlotta stumbled into his friend, and then he popped me on the ass when I went by. Fuckin' pig!"

With the tap on his phone, Leo called LSI-WC. "We're on the road. Natalie just identified the man from the security." He listened for a few seconds, then added, "I'll pass that along." Turning toward her, he said, "Do you have the man's face on the screen right now?"

"Yep. Front and center."

"Okay, just leave it there. Jeb can tap into your phone and see the screen exactly as you have it."

As a part of a Delta support team, she'd had access to a lot of special equipment for running intel quickly. She was used to working with programs that most people only thought would appear in fiction or movies. But until Leo started working for LSI-WC, she had no idea the scope that the private sector could work with. Letting her phone rest in her lap with the man's face staring up at her, she kept her gaze pinned on it. Narrow head, tanned complexion, black hair swept neatly back, dark eyes, and the gold incisor crown was shining as though taunting her. So focused on memorizing every detail, she jumped slightly when Jeb's voice came through Leo's speaker.

"Fuckin' fantastic, Natalie! We're running this through the databases now, and I'll let you know as soon as we get a hit. Report in once you're at the destination."

"Roger that," she mouthed as Leo spoke the words aloud. How many times in the field had she heard him give and receive commands? And while she'd befriended and protected everyone on their former team, she couldn't deny that he was the one whose actions had been memorized. Glancing to the side, she caught him looking her way and their eyes met. For the first time, she was uncertain what thoughts lay behind his gaze. Licking her suddenly dry lips, she forced a smile on her face before looking back down at her phone, pretending to be fascinated with the face of the man they were after.

She couldn't remember ever avoiding Leo's gaze before. But she kept her face diverted, afraid that he'd see that she wanted him in ways beyond friendship.

"I'll give that to you for now," he said, his voice both firm and soft.

She jerked her head up and around to stare, but he

was focused on driving with his eyes facing the wind-shield, giving her nothing to go on other than his words. It was on the tip of her tongue to ask him what he meant, but uncertainty kept her mouth closed. Quietly releasing a long breath, she wondered what was happening between her and her best friend.

"Got it," Carson said over the speaker, drawing her attention back to the mission. She inwardly cursed at her scattered thoughts, something that had never happened on a mission before.

"Bastion Trejo. At least that's the name he goes by, but we're uncertain if that's his birth name or not. He's part of the Sinaloa cartel and manages the casino you were at the other night, undoubtedly running drug money through the business."

"So was this all coincidence? Which, by the way, I don't believe in," she huffed. "There's no way he could have known I would be witness to the assassination."

"It could be that when he saw you, he assumed Carlotta was with you and sent someone to grab her."

"So why would he want to take Carlotta? We still don't know that he took Abril. If we go on the assumption that he meant to take Carlotta instead of Abril, I still don't understand why. He's powerful. Wealthy. And risking a helluva lot trying to kidnap an American actress," Natalie wondered aloud.

"The cartels are into a fuck of a lot besides drugs. They'll run human trafficking, and I imagine that someone with a big name could bring a lot of money and not ransom."

A shiver ran through Natalie, and her stomach

dropped. "Oh God. And when he realizes he doesn't have Carlotta, but he has a Guatemalan *look-alike*? What happens to Abril then?"

"Let's not get ahead of ourselves," Leo warned, glancing to the side.

Carson agreed. "Absolutely. Don't get ahead of yourself. Don't make assumptions. We have no idea if he was actually after Carlotta. We're still looking into Abril's family and their connections. There could be some reason he or someone else from the cartel took her as his true target. Maybe to have leverage with her family for some reason."

She scrunched her brow, pinching her lips together as thoughts crowded her mind until Leo interrupted.

"We're almost to the resort near the casino. We'll check in and get back in touch with you to see what our next move should be. My vote is that I get into the casino as a tourist and search."

"I understand the necessity for moving fast, but I'd rather you wait until Rick gets there. As soon as we have an ETA for him, we'll let you know."

Leo disconnected the call, then glanced over at Natalie again. This time, she had no problem reading his thoughts as she recognized his serious expression during planning. That was an expression she was used to seeing. Breathing a little easier, she looked ahead as he pulled through the lush, palm tree–lined drive to the resort's reception area. He parked, and they climbed from the vehicle at the same time, meeting at the front.

"Ready to play Mr. and Mrs. Parker?"

Nodding, she placed her hand dramatically on her

chest, fluttered her eyelashes, and quipped, "Just what I've always wanted to do, buddy boy."

He laughed and wrapped his arm around her neck, pulling her playfully to him. An easy, joking maneuver they'd enacted numerous times over the years. Yet, this time, her pulse beat faster, and her palms grew sweaty.

And adding in the idea of portraying a married couple, even for a day, now made her chest ache as her heart squeezed.

14

The drive had been torturous. Leo swallowed a groan as they pulled into the resort's parking lot. When Natalie had thrown open the door of her crappy hotel room, his eyes had drunk her in, both to assure himself that she was okay but also in acknowledgment that every inch of her was committed to memory. Dark hair pulled up haphazardly. Black T-shirt tucked into dark jeans. And her boots.

And when she'd leaped into his arms, he'd held her tighter than he ever had before. The feeling of her pressed against him was almost overwhelming. It struck him that she was showing need, something she rarely did. Also, the fact that she was obviously as glad to see him as he was to see her did not go unnoticed. The realization that with her body pressed to his, it felt so right. There was no way he mistook the way her body responded to his any more than he could try to hide his physical need for her. But more than that, he was sure their heartbeats synchronized.

Having to spend almost two hours in the car while she pored over her video clips and pictures and while keeping their conversation professional, considering LSI-WC was on the line, almost drove him mad. All he wanted to do was pull to the side of the road, drag her over the console and onto his lap, and kiss her until she would have no doubt their friendship was changing.

"Ready to play Mr. and Mrs. Parker?" The unrehearsed words slid from his mouth, and he had no idea where the idea came from. He knew reservations would have been made for two rooms, but the words popped out, and Natalie rolled with them, her typical sarcasm bursting forth, easing whatever tension might have crept between them.

He dragged her into their familiar, side-by-side walk where his arm rested on her shoulders, and he pulled her closer, only it felt more intimate this time. Knowing he needed to get them inside, registered, and in their room so they could keep planning the mission, he tamped down the swirling emotions that had never plagued him during a mission before.

The resort she had stayed in while working for Carlotta had been a four-star hotel, but this one was definitely a three, maybe a two. But for a third-world country, it was more than adequate. *And we won't be here long.* Leading her to the reception desk, he registered, barely catching the long gaze the receptionist sent toward him after she'd looked Natalie up and down. Natalie's hair was pulled into a ponytail, and her face was makeup-free. It was easy to see from the receptionist's face that she didn't consider his *wife* to be competition and had smiled encouragingly up at him. Not giving her the time of day, he signed the forms and paid quickly. His focus centered on Natalie as she glanced around the room filled with potted plants and a small bubbling fountain in the corner. Grabbing the keys, he walked back and pulled her close to him, kissing the top of her head. She bestowed a smile on him, then relaxed in his arms.

They had left their luggage in the SUV and walked back to the parking lot to grab what they needed. Natalie unzipped her bags and moved a few things around, only bringing the smallest one as well as her purse. He wasn't surprised. *She always did pack light.* Plus, as former military, he'd seen her make do with very little.

A flash of memory hit him of a woman he'd dated for a couple of months several years ago. It had taken forever for her to get ready, but when he'd looked at her perfect hair and makeup, he'd thought it had been worth it. But the longer they dated, the more irritated he became that they could never get anywhere on time. Her idea of her perfect looks began to chafe, and he found her more complicated than his interest could warrant. Natalie could pull off a night on the town, hike up a mountain, or lounge on a Sunday morning to perfection with very little effort. *Just one more woman in a line of women who couldn't hold a candle to my Nat.*

Jerking back to the present, he grabbed his duffel and leaned down to grab her bag as well, but she beat him to it. Waggling her finger back and forth, she grinned. "Hubby dear, you know I always handle my own luggage."

"Yeah, but I'm not making my wife drag her suitcase around, so hand it over, tough girl."

She glared and then huffed, handing him her bag. "I don't know if I want to be married to you if you're gonna be so bossy."

"Oh, come on, sweetie pie," he cajoled. "You know you're gonna love being married to me—umph!" The grunt left his lips as she elbowed him in the ribs.

He loved seeing her smile, then noted as it slowly left her face. Understanding her mood, he nodded. "Let's get to the room, and then we can get in touch with LSI-WC. We'll find out what our next step needs to be in locating Abril." With that, he led the way down a palm-lined path to their small villa. Opening the door, he stepped in first and shot his gaze over the small but neat room, taking in the floral sofa and chair facing a television on one side and a tiny kitchenette with a round bar table and two stools on the other. Two doors were at the back of the room.

"This looks awfully small for a two-bedroom suite," she said, shifting around him and moving into the room.

As he set their luggage on the floor, he looked over as she threw open one door and peered in, calling out, "This is the bathroom."

He reached the other door at the same time and could easily see that it was only one bedroom with one bed. Looking over his shoulder toward the sofa, understanding hit. "They consider the sleeper sofa out here to be another bedroom."

She turned slowly, her eyes lifted to his, but he had no idea what she was thinking. He lost all sense of time as they stood a foot apart, her head leaned back, and his chin bent so that their gazes stayed on each other. *One bedroom. One bed.* That wasn't what he assumed they were getting, but fuck if he could come up with a reason they should request something different. And if the slight hitch in her breath was anything to go by, she couldn't either.

Pulled by an invisible magnet, he leaned forward as she lifted on her toes. When their mouths were inches apart, his phone vibrated, the sound causing them to jerk back as though a crash of cymbals reverberated through the room.

Grabbing his phone from his pocket, his voice was hoarse as he growled, "Talk to us." Hitting the speaker button, he turned and set it on the table.

As though wanting to get as close as possible, Natalie put her foot on the rail of the barstool and hefted herself into the seat, her legs dangling as she leaned on her elbows, her attention focused on his phone. Blinking, he forced his thoughts off her and back to the mission.

"Okay, first the man Natalie saw. Bastion Trejo," Jeb began. "Thirty-two years old and already obtained a position of trust and responsibility in the cartel. While not exactly a rags-to-riches tale, he didn't come from the upper echelon. His father and uncles managed and oversaw several opium farms and packing facilities. His father was forward-thinking enough to make sure Bastion didn't drop out of school and just work at a low-level position. He stayed in school to finish his education. He had a head for numbers and did well in business classes. With his family's push, it didn't take much for him to get a position at one of the casinos that the cartel uses to launder money. Within five years, he was managing the entire operation and doing so successfully. From all reports, the cartel trusts him, affording him money, power, and prestige. He can walk among the high rollers at the casino with a smile on his face, shaking their hands, but he'd order their execution in a heartbeat if necessary. He's on the radar of the ineffective Guatemalan drug task force and their national police, but no one will touch him."

Natalie grimaced. "Of course, Carlotta would have to trip into someone like him." Sighing, she added, "And it didn't help that he got handsy, and I got pissed."

Carson added, "I've got a contact with the US Department of State's Bureau of International Narcotics and Law enforcement affairs. The INL has programs with Guatemala to fight corruption, drug trafficking, gang violence, arms trafficking, and human trafficking, but they face challenges. There are simply too many areas of the country under the cartels' influence. They want Bastion taken down—"

"But what about Abril's kidnapping?" Natalie blurted. "I mean, this Bastion Trejo is a big, bad dude, and I get that the Guatemalan police would like to get him for assassinating some poor bloke on the street, which means they'd like to have my eyewitness account, but all I care about is Abril!"

"We're getting to that," Carson admonished.

Natalie winced and mumbled, "Sorry. Go on."

Jeb jumped back into the conversation. "The tag on the vehicle that took Abril is part of a fleet of vehicles owned by the casino run by Bastion."

"Shit… the assassination and the kidnapping are related… at least by the perpetrator," she whispered, her gaze jumping up to Leo's. "That asshole has her."

He reached over and took her hand, holding it tightly, hoping to infuse warmth into her suddenly cold fingers.

Carson came back onto the line. "It wasn't just any poor bloke who was gunned down, but the grandson of a Zeta drug lord, not part of the Sinaloa cartel. His grandfather and father are currently in prison. It is being considered that the grandson was trying to take over his own corner of the drug transportation in the area, and Bastion was authorized to neutralize him in a public way that would leave no doubt in the minds of anyone else who had such aspirations."

"Shit," Leo muttered, leaning back in his seat with his hand still holding Natalie's.

"I hate to ask what I already know is a stupid question, but what about the Guatemalan police?" Natalie asked.

Another Keeper jumped in. "This is Chris. I've been looking at the info on the cartels' activities in Guatemala. The police are ineffective in most areas of keeping down the DTOs– drug trafficking organizations. Also, because of the multitude of other cartel activities such as kidnapping, extortion, arms trafficking, illegal adoption rings, and environmental crimes such as logging, illegal fisheries, and thefts of rare artifacts, just to name a few. These flourish in Guatemala."

Leo held Natalie's gaze, and she shook her head, whispering, "My fucking head is about to explode. These people have Abril."

Her voice broke on the last word, and he slid her stool toward his, wrapping his arm around her. She dropped her head onto his shoulder, and he held her as they continued to listen.

"This is Adam. Continuing the bad news, active and former military members are a big part of the problem. They run illicit organizations that allow the cartels from being caught and dealt with. The permissive and often complicit police force is mostly poorly paid and poorly educated, easily deciding to assist the cartels when faced with the option of death if they don't."

"So we'll get no assistance from them when looking for Abril," Leo surmised.

Carson said, "Through a knowledgeable contact, I've communicated with one of the high-level narcotics detectives in the Guatemalan police force that has not been bought out. Now, my contact trusts this man completely. There are others on his team, but I'm reluctant to draw too many people into the mission. I prefer to keep it with my Keepers and this one Guatemalan detective."

Leo and Natalie shared a look as silent messages moved between them. He could tell that, like him, she preferred not to trust anyone outside their circle, but Leo put his faith in Carson. She pinched her lips, her expression hard, then she finally nodded. Breathing easier, he turned his attention back to his phone.

"Right now, boss, I see this as a rescue mission for Abril De la Cruz. I want to find her, get her to safety, then get Natalie the fuck out of this country. If getting rid of a drug-kingdom killer like Bastion happens at the same time, all the better, but that's not my goal."

"Absolutely," Carson agreed. "The contact I spoke to is Detective Alarico Ortiz. He's actually a police commander, and while he plays a neutral part to keep down the cartel suspicions, he is a tireless worker behind the scenes with a small group of others he trusts."

"Shit," Natalie murmured, shaking her head. "If he really is who he says he is, as soon as anyone gets an idea that he's one of the good guys, then he's got a price on his head, a target on his back, and people gunning for him every second of the day."

"I've got no problem giving him whatever intel we get," Leo said, "but it's secondary to rescuing Abril and getting Natalie out of here."

Natalie glared up at him. "Would you stop acting like I'm some damsel in distress!"

"That's not what I'm saying. I'm just making the point that I have no intentions of turning this into a cartel takedown."

"If all I wanted was to get on the plane to get out of here, I could've done that at any time—"

Leo threw up his hands. "Look, Nat—"

"Okay, the two of you," Carson interrupted. "Keep your spat to yourself and focus on finding Abril."

Leo felt his face warm with his boss's rebuke. "Sorry." Breathing deeply, he continued, "What do we know about the casino? Do you think that's the place where they took Abril?"

"Possibly. Dolby and Poole have been going through the security videos outside the casino to see if the identified SUV came in. The problem is that a lot of dark SUVs are in the vicinity, and not all entrances have camera video. They don't have street cameras, so we can't follow anyone other than just looking at what's on the building."

"Can we go in?" Natalie asked. "Go in as tourists and look around?"

"We need to wait until after dark. By then, Rick and our Guatemalan contact will be there with more equipment."

An expression of terror moved over Natalie's face, and Leo reached over to take her hand, giving it a squeeze. He knew exactly what she was thinking. *The longer they go before they can look, find, and rescue Abril, the more time someone has to hurt her.*

"I know this sucks, Natalie," Carson acknowledged. "Keep in mind that this was not just snatching a random female from the road. This was in daylight and with a woman who had been in the company of and looks very much like an American actress. They are not gonna risk harming her in any way before trying to ransom her."

"Yes, but they don't have Carlotta. When they realize they don't, what will they do to Abril?"

"We've been following Bastion, and he left the scene of the assassination and came straight back to the casino. Odds are, he hasn't seen Abril yet, so she'll be safe for now. But Natalie, rushing a mission without all the intel only puts the two of you at risk. I know you care for Abril, but with your background, you know I'm right."

She sighed heavily and nodded. "Yeah, I do. I don't mean to sound ungrateful."

Leo squeezed her hand again as Carson replied, "You don't sound ungrateful. You sound exactly like what I would expect from any one of my Keepers... ready to jump in to protect and save."

Carson's words struck Leo straight in the heart, and he shot his gaze toward Natalie, watching as pride curved her lips upward ever so slightly. Clearing his throat, he looked back down for the phone. "Have Jeb send us any information he has on the casino, plus Nat has been there, so we'll have her memories, as well."

"Will do. Just so you know, Hop will get Rick close to you in a small private airstrip that we know is clean, not cartel-owned. He will be met by Alarico, and the two of them will come to where you are. Hop will stay with the plane. Their ETA is probably about four hours away."

With that, they disconnected the call. He leaned back in his chair, keeping his gaze on Natalie. Her brow was furrowed, evidence of her mind racing through various scenarios of what was upcoming. He leaned closer and dragged his forefinger along the crease on her forehead. "If you keep thinking so hard, you'll get wrinkles."

Scowling, she quipped, "Why, hubby dear, you were supposed to love me even if I do get wrinkles."

Barking out a laugh, he slid from the stool and, before she had a chance to protest, moved to stand next to her, his thighs between her knees. Even on the tall stool, she was still shorter, but he'd always loved the way she fit when next to him. He placed one hand on the table next to her and the other on the back of her seat, effectively boxing her in. If she wanted space, all she'd have to do was ask. He also knew if she wanted to make a point, she could easily knee him in the balls.

His gaze held hers, and his breath caught in his throat as he waited to see if she would protest, crack a joke, throw a glare, or continue to stare up at him with the specter in her eyes that made him think she was feeling the same thing he did.

She didn't make him wait long as her hands lifted, and she grasped his shoulders. As he leaned forward, he lifted his hand from her chair and glided his fingers over her shoulder, cupping the back of her neck. He angled her head with his thumb gently under her chin, and her fingers dug in tighter to his shoulders. Their lips met, the kiss slow and soft. *Christ!* He'd kissed many women in his life, but his memory short-circuited, and he couldn't remember anyone other than the woman in front of him. The scent of the minty gum she'd chewed earlier teased his nostrils, and he couldn't wait to taste her deeper. He angled his head, and the slight motion had her shift on her seat, pulling herself closer. The position was perfect for gliding his tongue over hers and sweeping through her mouth, her minty taste teasing his taste buds.

As her tongue tangled with his, all the blood rushed from his head to his cock, and he shifted his stance to ease the pressure. Time ceased to exist as the kiss continued, but after starting slow and gentle, flames now shot between them, and he could feel the fiery burn of passion. Heads twisted, noses bumped, and his arms now banded around her back, pulling her tight so that her breasts crushed against his chest. They'd hugged countless times in the past, but he'd always blanked his mind to the feel of her in his arms. Now, every inch of his body was wired as sensations battled for supremacy. Her lithe, athletic body as it wiggled closer. Her breasts he'd so often tried not to stare at in the past when barely covered by her bikini. Her mouth, lips, and tongue had become a drug he wasn't sure he could live without.

Still standing between her legs as she sat on the barstool, her heat was pressed against his erection. He jutted his hips forward, not hiding the bulge she could easily feel as the desire to lose himself in her took hold. She looped her arms around his neck at the same time her legs wrapped around his waist. The deft move caught him by surprise, but with her once again in his arms, he held her tight as he stood straight, and she clung to him, the kiss never breaking.

For once, Leo had no plan. He'd expected them to work the mission and have a conversation about wanting more than just friendship. He'd imagined a rational discourse, but that concept was now blown out of the water as neither seemed to be able to get enough of each other's bodies.

He turned to stalk toward the bedroom, then halted. *Shit, what if this isn't what she wants? What if this is just a kiss and nothing more? I'd meant for us to talk everything over before we—*

"Are you gonna think, or are we gonna fuck?" Natalie mumbled against his lips just before her tongue tangled with his once again.

Her words had the effect she must have wanted because his cock swelled even more, and his feet hurried to carry them into the bedroom. She was still in his arms with their lips still locked together. All the smooth moves he'd used before fled from his mind. *Lay her on the bed? Drop her feet to the floor and let her slide down my front? Strip her first, or let her strip for me? Shit, this is my best friend...*

As his mind raced through possibilities, he felt the loss of her mouth as she leaned back and pinned him with a hard stare.

"If you think this much all the time, I'm surprised you ever get laid!"

Blinking, he barked out a laugh as the uncertainties melted away.

15

Natalie swam in uncharted waters, but with the jolts of electricity flying between her and Leo, singeing every nerve in her body, she was ready to dog paddle across the ocean if necessary.

She was trained and used to the unexpected, which was good, considering the day's events had not gone according to plan. Right now, she would already have landed in LA if she'd gotten on her plane this morning. But from the impromptu coffee invite from Abril, witnessing an assassination in the street, recognizing one of the assassins, Abril's kidnapping, and consulting with LSI-WC, her day had been shocking, to say the least. But most of all, it was the kiss with her best friend, the man she cared for more than anyone else and had compared every other man she dated with and found them lacking, that shot her straight to the middle of the ocean without a life jacket. And while terrified, she was consumed with drowning in the sensations and not wanting them to stop.

If the bulge nestled against her crotch was anything to go by, Leo was definitely *into* the kiss and just as affected as she was. But he was hesitating, and she didn't have to guess why. Leo was top-notch at analyzing missions, and while she was also scared of what they both wanted, she was more scared of him backing off and walking away.

Calling him on it, she grinned when he barked out a laugh. Leo was always handsome, whether cool and collected for a night on the town or hot and sweaty coming in from training or a mission. But laughing? He was fuckin' gorgeous.

As his laughter slowly subsided, their eyes remained locked. Still holding his arms, she waited. Whatever happened between them was going to have to come from him. Time seemed to stand still, and she felt light-headed from holding her breath.

Finally, he said, "I don't want to fuck this up, but I want you."

Terrified of misreading the situation, she pressed her lips together for a moment, then asked, "Just tell me this… do you want *a* woman, or do you want *me*?"

His jaw hardened, and his eyes narrowed. "You know me better than that, Nat."

He was right. She did. Leo never did anything rash or unfeeling. Nodding slowly, she agreed. "Yeah, I do." There were no sounds in the room other than the ticking of an old clock on the nightstand next to the bed and the birds chirping outside the window. And still, she waited.

His arms continued to hold her tightly as he moved

toward the bed. He bent forward until her ass was settled, and she loosened her legs from around his waist. He stood, and with her hands propped on the mattress behind her, she leaned her head way back to continue to hold his gaze. The intensity filled the room, and just when she was afraid that he might back away, his hand lifted to grasp the material of his T-shirt behind his neck.

As he dragged it up, she watched as each delectable inch of skin was exposed before he pulled his shirt over his head and tossed it to the chair next to the bed. *How many times have I seen him shirtless? Traced his tattoos with my eyes? Memorized each one as he told me their meanings? Watched him working out or playing with the other team members, each muscle flexing under smooth, tanned skin?* The answer was countless times, yet right now, she felt as though she needed to re-memorize the sight.

Her gaze caught and lingered on the puckered scar on his shoulder. *I remember that, too. Listening to the team as gunfire erupted, like so many missions before. But that time, hearing that Leo had been hit, her lungs had refused to work, holding her breath captive. She'd forced her mind to stay on the mission. Forced her heart to keep beating. Forced air in and out until they'd received the report that he was going to be fine and the team was coming in. When she'd seen him upon his return, all patched up with his arm in a sling, she knew what she felt was more than what she'd ever willingly admitted before. Oh, she'd kept it a secret. Still pretending and joking and giving the impression that they were only friends. But when a heart threatens to break at the idea of another person never coming home, then...*

So lost in thought as she stared at his chest that when he bent forward, she jumped slightly. With the top of his head in front of her face as he leaned over to pull off his boots, she reached out and ran her fingers through his thick curls. At her touch, he looked up and grinned. There was nothing boyish about Leo's face, yet he looked so pleased that she wondered what he must've looked like when he was a child.

Standing again, he toed off his boots. With his hands resting on his trim hips, his gaze ran over her, and her body warmed under his perusal. Self-confidence had never been a problem for her, yet as her hands moved to drag her shirt upward, the memory of seeing some of his past dates hit her. Leo had never had a specific type of woman who held his attention, yet she'd occasionally seen him with tall, elegant women with manicured nails, expertly applied makeup, and salon-worthy hair that would've cost Natalie a week's rent.

"Now who's overthinking?"

Rolling her eyes at his comment, she jerked her shirt over her head and tossed it straight toward him. His hand reached up, grabbing it before it hit him in the face. Still grinning, he dropped it into the chair on top of his. Her hands moved to the bottom of her sports bra, finding the breathable cotton to be much more comfortable and supportive than a fancy, lacy bra. Part of her wished she had something more attractive, but considering he'd seen her in a sports bra as they were running together, she didn't think he'd care. Plus, it was her experience that bras would only stay on for a moment, fancy or not. What most men wanted to see was naked breasts anyway.

He reached out, and his hand stilled hers before sliding his fingers underneath the elastic band. Drawing it carefully over her breasts, he began pulling it upward. She lifted her arms over her head, and he continued to peel the bra off, allowing it to join their shirts on the chair.

She kept her gaze on his face, pleased to see the flare in his eyes as his attention focused on her breasts. She didn't need to look down to know her nipples were erect. He bent and placed each hand next to her hips on the bed, bringing his face toward her chest. Arching her back, she offered herself to him.

He wrapped his lips around her nipple, his tongue circling the bud before sucking gently. She'd always felt cheated in the past when a man considered a few nipple pinches as the extent of foreplay, but with just Leo's mouth barely sucking, she was ready to come.

He moved slowly from one breast to the other, and she continued to arch her back in silent invitation for him to taste his fill. He did not disappoint. He lifted his hand and placed it on her shoulder, applying slight pressure so that she fell back onto the bed. His fingers moved to the front of her pants, deftly undoing the buttons and zipper. She lifted her ass to assist as he slid her pants and panties down her legs.

When they tangled at her booted feet, he seemed surprised that he'd forgotten that she still had shoes on. It took him a moment to deal with her boots, then he finished undressing her.

Now lying completely nude on the bed, it was difficult to drag in air as she stared at his face while his gaze devoured her. He'd seen her in a bikini numerous times before, but laid bare before him was different. They had already crossed an invisible threshold to a place they'd never been, and she instinctively knew they could never go backward. She should have been terrified, yet she prayed he wanted to go forward as much as she did.

With his gaze still on her, his hands went to his belt. The sound of the leather sliding through the buckle and then the click of the zipper sent a shiver over her body. His pants and boxers soon joined the pile of clothing on the chair.

Dragging her gaze over his muscular body, focusing her attention on his impressive erection, the air rushed from her lungs. *Christ Almighty!* Was there anything about his body that wasn't perfect? He was well endowed, and she had no doubt he knew how to wield his cock for maximum pleasure. She'd never been the jealous type before, but then she'd never had a man who inspired that emotion. Right now, looking at Leo in all his glory, she wished she could go back and cut out the eyes of any woman who'd had the privilege of seeing him naked. But then, realizing she would benefit from his experience, she thought perhaps sending a thank-you card to his previous partners might be in order.

"I'd give anything to know what you're thinking right now," he said.

Blinking up at him, she grinned. "I was just thinking that you're mighty impressive to look at, and I hope to God you know what to do with that thing," she said, inclining her head toward his cock. "Because I sure as hell know a few things I'd like to do."

He laughed again, and her grin widened. He reached over and jerked his wallet from his pants, pulling out a condom and tossing it on the bed next to her. He dropped to his knees, pushing her thighs apart with his wide shoulders. "Don't worry, Nat. I know what I'm doing."

She couldn't wait to feel his mouth on her, but he hesitated, blowing his breath over her heated flesh first.

Holding her gaze, he said, "Believe me when I say I know what I'm doing. And if you try to leave this bed before we have a chance to talk when it's all over, I'll tie you down, even if I have to tell Rick to wait outside when he gets here." Before she had a chance to retort, he licked her folds, and all thoughts shot from her mind. Her hands found his hair, and her fingers burrowed in his curls as her short nails dragged along his scalp. He licked and sucked, his mouth working miracles. He shifted and thrust a finger inside her core while circling his tongue around her swollen bud.

Her hips writhed, lifting to offer more of herself to him. Her body seemed to flame as jolts of electricity moved through her nerves. Just when she wasn't sure if she could take another moment of this sweet torture, she flung her head back as her inner sex quivered around his fingers. Her release swept over her, and she lay boneless, her legs flopped apart like a frog, heedless of her unsexy position and inability to think of something flirty and coy to say.

He crawled over her body, and when his hands were

by her head and his hips nestled between her thighs, he lay down and kissed her again thoroughly. She wasn't sure she could catch her breath but wasn't about to complain, losing herself in the sensations.

Against her lips, he mumbled, "I think I finally found something that keeps you from coming up with a smart-ass comment."

"Shut up," she mumbled in return, continuing the kiss.

"Is that the best you can come up with?"

Pushing against his shoulders so that the kiss ended as he was lifted an inch above her, she raised a brow. "Shut up and fuck me."

A flare of lust moved through his eyes, and his lips curved slowly. "We're going to do this, Natalie, but this is no fuck. With you, babe, it's never just a fuck."

Before she had a chance to ponder those words or consider what they were doing and how it would affect their friendship, or maybe even push him away, he grabbed the condom and rolled it on, then lined the tip of his cock at her entrance.

And then, being the man that he was, he waited. This amazing, smart, best friend man. His dick had to be ready to explode, but he waited to give her the ultimate say in the decision. It could've made her feel powerful, but instead, she was humbled by the gift he was handing her, just like all the gifts he'd ever bestowed upon her, especially his friendship. Whatever came tomorrow, she wanted this with him now.

"Yes," she said, handing the gift back to him. He pressed his hips forward and entered her body, stealing her breath. And if she was honest, he'd just stolen her heart, as well.

———

Leo battled to keep his eyes open as he sent his cock deep into Natalie's sweet sex. Part of him wanted to close his eyes to blank out everything but the sensations of the woman who meant the world to him. But then he instantly knew that he wanted to take in every experience he was feeling.

The smell of her release was intoxicating. Her penetrating and trusting dark-eyed gaze held him captured. The taste of her was still on his tongue. Her short breaths and little gasps filled his ears. And her tight inner muscles gripped his cock. He was overwhelmed and humbled. This was Natalie. His Nat. Best friend extraordinaire. Fun, smart, witty. The most beautiful woman he'd ever seen.

As he thrust deeper into her body, he wondered why they'd never previously crossed this line. But before he had a chance to ponder the answer to that thought, his brain short-circuited to anything other than offering and receiving pleasure. He shifted his position so that he not only drove his cock as deep as possible but also swept over her sensitive bud. Pants of air burst from her lungs.

Dropping to his forearms, he kissed her deeply, driving his tongue into her mouth. He wasn't going to last but refused until she came with him. Kissing along her jaw, he dragged his tongue down and sucked a nipple, moving between breasts. "Are you close?" he groaned, each word pulled from deep inside his chest.

She nodded in reply, but he needed to make a change so that he didn't come too quickly. Shoving his hands under her back, he rolled, flipping them. Now with her on top, she shifted so that her knees were on either side of his hips. Looking down, she grinned.

"Ride me," he ordered.

"With pleasure." Her eyes lit, and her smile widened.

With her hands on his shoulders, she shifted her body up and down on his cock, fast and slow, until he thought he would go mad with longing. With one hand on her breasts, rolling her nipple between his forefinger and thumb, his other hand shifted down to the bundle of nerves where their bodies were joined. Her fingers dug into his shoulders as she threw her head back and cried out her release.

Her sex squeezed his cock, and he grabbed her hips and lifted her slightly so he could piston deeper. Now giving over to all the sensations, he lifted his knees to support her back as he roared through his orgasm, allowing her body to milk his until every drop was wrung from him.

Watching them come together had been the greatest emotional as well as sexual experience of his life. He barely had time to get ready before she flopped forward, landing on his chest, eliciting a grunt as the air rushed from his lungs. They lay for several long minutes, their breaths and heartbeats slowing. Hands drifted over shoulders and backs as they rolled to face each other.

He knew he needed to take care of the condom but

didn't want to leave her just yet, afraid she'd start over-thinking— or underthinking what they'd just experienced together. He rolled to one side of the bed, taking her with him. Standing, he lifted her in his arms and stalked to the bathroom.

"What are you doing—"

"I don't want to be separated," he explained. He was ready for her to argue but was surprised and grateful when she didn't. Setting her on the counter, he dealt with the condom before leaning around to wash his hands. Gathering her in his arms again, they moved back into the bedroom. Leaning over, he tugged down the covers before placing her gently in the bed and climbing in next to her. Pulling her close, he held her tightly, her cheek pressed over his heartbeat, then kissed the top of her head.

Her hair was sex-messed but soft against his finger-tips as he threaded his fingers through her tresses. "We need to talk."

She leaned back so that their eyes could meet. Seeing uncertainty move through her brown eyes, he plunged ahead, not wanting to let her doubt his feelings for another second.

"You're my best friend."

She blinked at his pronouncement, a crinkle forming between her brows.

Rushing ahead, he continued. "It's not just that you're smart, funny, and hold your own in poker and pool. It's not just that you can plan a mission, sort through intel, and analyze situations faster than any other support member I've ever worked with. It's not just that you can kick ass and take down a man much larger than your-self, are a superior marksperson with every weapon I've ever seen you fire, and can rock a bikini while looking equally sexy in jeans and boots. It's not just that you've put up with my shit for years, called me out when I'm an ass, and made me want to be a better man. It's all those things wrapped up together in someone who has shown me what true loyalty and friendship are for years."

She blinked again. This time, her mouth opened slightly, and her eyes widened. He couldn't help but grin, knowing he'd shocked her into silence.

"I also know that we just burned up the sheets, and that was just the tip of what I know we can do together. I wondered why we'd never crossed this line before, but I figure there's a right time for everything. For all these years, we've built a friendship, trust, a relationship based on everything except sex. Nat, babe, we're solid. My other friends have always wondered why we never got together, but I still think it comes down to timing. And this is our time for starting what will take a lifetime to enjoy."

"Uh…" She pressed her lips together, her gaze never leaving his.

"Do you disagree with anything I said?"

Her lips quivered, and she swallowed deeply. "I remember the first time I met you."

He jerked slightly, her words catching him by surprise.

"I'd already been on the support team and recently transferred to your unit. I barely had time to meet everyone when the mission came in, and I was thrust into the analysis. A few of you came in from training, and as soon as your eyes met mine when you walked into the room, something happened. Something I'd never felt before."

"What did you feel?"

She chewed on her lip for a moment, and he gave her time. One of the greatest gifts from Natalie was when she opened enough to bestow her thoughts to someone, and he was honored she'd done that many times over the years with him.

"You know my dad. Military tough. No room for anything but duty, honor, and orders. And ever since I'd been in the military, I tried to follow his creed. Being female, I knew I'd always be challenged. Being a petite female could only make things worse in that world. So I learned to be tough. But you took one look at me and grinned. Not a sexy grin like you thought I was there for your pleasure and were trying to get in my pants. Not a condescending grin like you thought I got the position just because I was female, and you were waiting for me to fuck up. It wasn't like that at all. It was just an open, friendly smile, and in that instant, I knew I wanted to know you better."

He ran his finger over her cheek, loving the soft feel of her skin. "I wanted the same thing."

"I've never given in to romantic musings, but I felt as though we were going to be close. I never imagined you would become my best friend, but your friendship came to mean everything to me."

"And you don't want to lose it." When she shook her head slowly, he assured, "I don't either, Natalie."

"But now? What if—"

Pressing his forefinger over her lips, he stilled her words. "There is no what-if. We've built a solid friendship. We're already in a deep, committed relationship. We are now ready to make this commitment. There is no more wondering what if."

"Leo, I have to have you in my life. I don't think I can exist without you."

"Nat, babe, we're friends first and always. That will never change, and that's exactly why our becoming a couple is what will make this work. What I need to know is, do you believe that, too, and do you trust me?"

She sucked in a deep breath through her nose before letting it out slowly, their gazes never wavering. Slowly, she nodded, and her lips curved as she lifted her hand and cupped his cheek. "Yes. I do believe you, and I trust you with all my heart."

Erasing the distance between them, he kissed her, rolling over her body. The kiss flamed once again, and he thanked God he had another condom in his wallet.

16

If there had been a rug in the small room, Natalie would have worn a hole in it. Waiting for Rick made her antsy, and she couldn't figure out why. Glancing out the window once again, she caught her reflection and stared. *Okay, I do know why.* For a female to succeed in a male-dominated business, she always needed to bring her A game. But it was hard to focus when she really wanted to either climb Leo like a spider monkey or toss him back into the bed.

Whirling, she paced back over to the door leading to the bedroom and glanced inside. The bed was made military tight. All clothes had been put back on, right down to their boots. She'd even convinced Leo to take the small bathroom trash bag with the used condoms and wrappers out to the dumpster. Once again satisfied there was no evidence of the fiery passion from earlier, she turned and started back across the living room.

"Will you please stop!" Leo ordered, looking up from his computer as he sat on the stool near the small table.

Huffing, she planted her knuckles on her hips and glared, but he didn't give her a chance to speak.

"Look, babe, there is no way Rick is going to walk in here and think anything went on other than you and me just hanging out."

Stomping toward him, she poked him in the chest with her forefinger. "Babe? You slip up and call me *babe* in front of him, and he'll know something was going on."

"Christ, Nat, I'm not going to slip up. Plus, *babe* doesn't necessarily have to mean anything."

Her brows shot upward. "Oh, and that's supposed to make me feel better? You use a throwaway endearment for me that you've used for countless other females who have crossed your path?"

He leaned closer, his face right in front of hers. "How many times have you heard me refer to somebody as *babe* over the years?"

She huffed an exaggeration but knew the answer to that question. Leo truly was the steadiest man she'd ever known. "Okay, fine. Never."

He reached up and wrapped his fingers around hers. "Right. You know you're different. You know you're special. But I've got to ask… what are you so afraid of?"

She pressed her lips together, thoughts flying through her mind. *Your coworkers not taking me seriously. We have a mission to plan, and my brain is scattered. A woman I grew to care about was kidnapped, and we were burning up the sheets.*

He twisted in his seat to face her fully, his hands

drawing her closer between his legs. As though he could read her thoughts, he said, "Look, Natalie, you're not some conquest to me. There's no way I'll say or do anything that would embarrass you or demean what we did. You've been around Rick before. He likes you, thinks you're the shit, and could never understand why we weren't more than just friends. At the right time, he'll know, but I've got no intentions of making some kind of announcement the minute he walks through the door. After what we did, it might seem a little hard to focus right now, but you're the best team analyzer I ever worked with. As soon as Rick gets here and we can move forward, everything will click into place. And if you're feeling guilty about Abril, don't. Running off half-cocked is a surefire way to fuck up any mission. You know that."

Right on cue, a hard rap of knuckles was heard against the door. Sliding from the stool, Leo bent and kissed her quickly, jolting her into action. With her head held high, she threw her shoulders back and followed him to the door.

Rick entered, and before she had a chance to react, he wrapped his arms around her and lifted her straight off the floor, giving her a little shake while kissing the top of her head.

"Christ, you're just like Leo's brother, Oliver!"

"Natalie, girl, you sure do know how to show a guy a good time!"

As he plopped her back down on the floor, she sucked in a quick breath, wondering how he knew anything, but he kept talking as he shook hands and back slapped Leo.

"Damn, she comes down here as a bodyguard to some rising star and ends up with an assassination and kidnapping! Hell, that's the kind of stuff us Keepers live for!"

Leo shook his head and glared. "Chill the fuck out, Rick. And remember, the girl who was kidnapped is someone Natalie considers to be a friend."

Rick whirled around to face her, his expression full of contrition. "Aw, Nat, I'm sorry. I'm just running my mouth, you know that."

She nodded and grinned. "I know, I know. It's all cool."

Rick glanced around before he brought his attention back to her. "I know it's been hard waiting for more intel to come in and for me to arrive. I'm sure you two have gone nuts while waiting."

Keeping her face blank, she hoped he couldn't see the heat infusing her face. "Uh…" Another man stepped up to the doorway, and she stiffened.

Rick waved him in as Leo shut the door behind him. "This is Detective Alarico Ortiz. Alarico, this is Leo and Natalie. Carson has given him the authority to work with us. While there are other trustworthy Guatemalans in law enforcement, Alarico works specifically to mitigate the cartels."

"Mitigate?" she asked, finding Rick's word choice interesting.

Alarico turned toward her and inclined his head

politely. "If Rick had said *eradicate*, you wouldn't have believed him. Nor would I. And I would be stuck in a job with no hope of ever attaining my goal."

Cocking her head to the side, she ran her assessing gaze over him. "You don't believe the cartels will ever be completely defeated."

Now it was his turn to pin her with his intelligent gaze. "No, I don't. Do you?"

Shaking her head slowly, she replied, "No. I fear evil and greed will always be with us, and so will those who don't care how they spread their evil or use their greed. And so you mitigate?"

"I do what I can to lessen their impact. Disrupt the flow of drugs. Create barriers for their cash flows. Try to find ways that farmers can continue to work their fields for legitimate crops. I believe the saying is 'hit them where it hurts.'"

Despite her reticence to trust anyone outside their inner circle, she couldn't help but smile. "If you can actually do any of those things, I believe you do hit them where it hurts."

"I thank you for your trust." He looked around at the others. "And now we focus on the casino and Bastion Trejo."

She glanced toward Leo, finding his assessing gaze pinned on her. For an instant, her mind tumbled to the change in their relationship, but with a minuscule shake of her head, she shoved those thoughts away. *Time to put away worry about Leo and me and move forward to find Abril.*

Driving to the casino, Leo sat in the back seat with Natalie, keeping his mind on the mission while keeping his eyes on her. When they'd checked into the resort, he hadn't planned on them falling into bed— or rather him carrying her off to bed like some hero on the cover of one of the old romance novels his mother used to read years ago.

He also knew it could have backfired horribly. Her worries about Abril. Accusing him of only thinking with his dick instead of about the mission. Taking advantage of the situation. But with nothing to do but wait until Rick arrived and the Keepers could send more intel to them, they'd given in to the urge they'd both been thinking about. And he had not one fuckin' regret and prayed she didn't either. Now, with the equipment Rick brought with him, they'd be able to get into the casino under cover of darkness and listen to Bastion's conversations without getting too close.

"And you're sure there's nothing else you can think of?" Alarico asked Natalie as he twisted around to look at her from the front seat.

Leo tensed as Natalie's brow lifted.

"You do know I'm a professional, right?" Natalie asked, her calm voice belying the tenor of irritation running through her words.

"Yes," Alarico said. "But even the most trained professional can think of something later when emotions are not running as high."

Leo wanted to reach over and take Natalie's hand

but didn't dare. He wouldn't do it to offer comfort because Natalie didn't need that. The desire was more to keep her from going ballistic on the unsuspecting police detective. But to do so could be misinterpreted by Alarico, and with the vibes rolling off Natalie, Leo was afraid he might lose his fingers. He hadn't even gotten around to mentioning to Natalie the idea of working for Carson and figured if they became coworkers and were in a relationship, there would be times when they would have to let each other work out their job frustrations. He looked up and caught Rick's grin in the rearview mirror and lifted his hand to pretend to cough as a cover for the snort of laughter ready to erupt.

"Because of my detailed observations and report, LSI-WC was able to identify a high-level Sinaloa cartel member and casino manager in the back seat of an SUV where the driver stopped in the middle of the road and shot a man before climbing from the vehicle, walking over, and assassinating him in cold blood. Also, because of my detailed observations and report, LSI-WC was able to trace this man back to the casino and follow a link to the vehicle that was used in the kidnapping of Abril De la Cruz." She cocked her head to the side and tapped her chin. "Oh, let's see... there's more! Because of my detailed observations and report, LSI WC has been able to verify the area where Bastion came from when I encountered him the other evening in the casino, giving them an excellent place to begin searching for information about his whereabouts."

Adopting a pseudo-coy expression, she batted her

eyelashes. "Gee, Detective Ortiz, do you think I've left anything out of my bubble head that must surely be used only for fixing my hair and makeup?"

Leo lost the battle to keep from laughing and was immediately joined by Rick's burst of laughter.

Natalie swung her head around and pierced him with a glare. "Well, am I wrong?"

Shaking his head, Leo said, "No, Nat, I'd say you made your point."

"Damn straight," Rick mumbled from the front seat.

The interior of the SUV was dark, but Leo was sure Alarico's face was probably burning from Natalie's ire. Thank God, the man knew when he'd been bested.

"Ms. Robinson, your point is well made. The details you provided have given us the chance to not only save Ms. De la Cruz but also get very close to taking down somebody we've been after for a while. I assure you that my questioning had nothing to do with your gender. My apologies."

Natalie leaned back and shrugged. "Apology accepted, but I should be gracious enough to say it's not necessary. Force of habit for me to be defensive, I suppose."

Leo relaxed, but his mirth came to a screeching halt as Natalie leaned forward again, her question to Alarico coming from out of the blue.

"Do you have a family? Are you married? Involved with someone?"

Leo's head whipped around, and his brows lowered in surprise. "Natalie, what the—"

She glanced toward Leo, then looked back at Alarico, who was holding her gaze as the air in the SUV seemed to thicken. "I would imagine that a man in your position would always be looking over his shoulder," she said.

"You would be right," Alarico said. "And no, I'm not married, nor am I involved with someone. Working on a relationship while constantly carrying out investigations and missions is very difficult. Plus, it makes me, and by association them, vulnerable."

"I'm sure it does." Her voice was soft.

Leo's heart pounded in his chest, hating for Natalie to think of a reason she and he shouldn't be together.

She glanced toward him, then turned to look out her window. "I suppose, with the right person, the reward is worth the risk."

Swallowing deeply, Leo glanced up to see Rick's penetrating gaze boring into him through the rearview mirror again. Wishing he could reach over and pull Natalie onto his lap, he fisted his hands on his thighs, barely breathing.

"Casino ahead," Rick said, effectively cutting off all further conversation.

Leo knew that Jeb and Chris had finally been able to tap into the casino security. With the cartel's money and the backing of some Guatemalan politicians and law enforcement, much of the casino was clouded in secrecy. As a place to launder money, they didn't follow any regulations or want to have a record of money changing hands.

Without the building's floor plan being electronically filed with any Guatemalan overseeing agency, they had to use what few cameras they could to tap into, along with Natalie's descriptions. Leo was incredibly proud of Natalie and thrilled to be working as a team again.

Once Rick parked on a side street near the casino, he and Rick moved to the back of the SUV. They'd given up on the idea of trying to go in as tourists visiting the casino, knowing that their size would automatically draw attention to themselves. Instead, dressed in all black with radio earpieces and recording equipment, they planned to slip in once it was dark and make their way to the roof, finding a way to slip inside the casino and get as close to Bastion's office as possible.

He looked over as Natalie sidled close to him, her head leaning back as her eyes searched his face. "What if she's not here? Just because the car that took her ended up here earlier doesn't mean she's still here."

"The Keepers are watching Bastion's known properties right now. But he owns several, and we save time if we can find out where he's going. This gives us the best chance of getting to the right place instead of wasting time running around looking."

She huffed, and he lost her eyes as she looked to the side. Nodding, she agreed. "I know you're right. It just seems like a lot of time has been wasted."

"Hey," he said, drawing her gaze back to him. "Think back to our Delta missions. How long would we plan some of those?"

"Sometimes for days, and that was even after the initial plan was given to us."

"Right. This one just feels different because you're personally involved with the victim."

Rick walked around Leo and bent to kiss the top of her head. "We got this. Thanks to you, we've got a fuck of a lot more intel than we ever could have gotten alone." Looking toward Leo, he asked, "You ready?"

With a dip of his chin, Leo answered, "Fuck yeah." Inclining his head toward the side where Alarico stood, Leo added, "Remember to behave yourself with him. Don't pick a fight. He's on our side."

She leaned closer and whispered, "Do you really trust him?"

Jerking slightly, he held back his quick acquiescence, then slowly nodded. "Let's just say that Carson doesn't have a reason not to trust him, and that's good enough for me for now."

She shook her head. "Carson doesn't really know him. Carson knows somebody who says he's trustworthy. That's not the same thing, Leo."

Leaning down, he placed his lips close to her ears. "The only people I would truly trust with my life or somebody I care about would be one of the Keepers or you. Since I can't leave you with one of them, and you'd probably kick me in the balls at the idea that you needed someone to babysit you, I'll just say, be careful. Keep your eyes and ears open, and don't let your guard down."

She grinned at his words. "So just keep being the badass you know that I am?"

"Abso-fucking-lutely." He wanted to lean down and kiss her but knew he couldn't. But held her gaze and hoped she knew he was thinking about how much he wanted to be with her. At the first opportunity, when they were alone, he fully intended to let her know exactly how he felt.

17

Leo stared at the back entrance of the casino, quickly noting it was not well guarded. He and Rick watched for a few minutes as kitchen employees went unchecked going in and out of the back door.

"Anybody can walk in," Rick commented.

"Yeah, but considering it's common knowledge that these casinos are run by the cartel, who would be stupid enough to try to sneak in?" He and Rick looked at each other, then grinned, bumping fists. Rounding the back corner, they easily found one of the fire escapes that appeared to have little use. The Keepers had already ascertained they were not on any security cameras.

Quickly ascending to the top of the three-story building, they made it onto the roof with no difficulty. Leo reported their progress by staying in contact with the Keepers and Natalie by radio.

"All looks normal on the public casino floor," Jeb said. "As well as the high-roller tables on the second floor."

There were no security cameras on the third floor, making it the perfect place for Bastion's office and any other room they wanted to keep secure.

"The bathrooms were on the far east side," Natalie recalled over the radio. "There was a hall that led from the casino to the employee area of the kitchen about twenty feet from the outer east wall. The stairs leading to the second floor were at the front entrance of that hall."

Noting the smaller bathroom windows on the first floor were exactly the same on the second and third, Leo glanced toward Rick. "The window on the third floor right below us is probably a bathroom, as well. Plumbing in a building like this would be simplistic."

"Agreed," Rick answered with a chin lift.

Close to the east side was a door leading from the roof to the third floor. Ascertaining it was close to the bathrooms and the supply closets, Leo and Rick prepared to override any locking mechanism and almost laughed when they discovered none. With Rick staying on the roof, Leo silently opened the door and stealthily moved down the stairs, halting at the doorway entrance to the third floor. With a snake camera, he observed a guard at the end of the hall whose stance was casual, giving evidence that his boss was not in the area.

Jeb's voice came over the radio again. "Bastion is moving through the first-floor casino. The man's got an eye for the ladies, and it looks like he could have his pick."

Leo's jaw tensed at the idea that Natalie had been

touched by that asshole. After another moment, he listened as Jeb added, "Bastion is starting up the stairs to the second floor where the high-roller tables are located."

With Bastion no longer in camera view, Leo continued to wait patiently. After several more minutes, the guard at the end of the hall snapped to attention. A few seconds later, Bastion and two flanking guards walked past the door leading to the roof before entering one of the rooms.

Slipping back up the stairs to the roof, Leo soundlessly closed the door behind him before reporting over the radio to Rick, the Keepers, and Natalie. "Bastion's office is on the third floor at the end of the hall on the north side."

Acting as a unit as finely tuned as the Deltas, he and Rick moved to the rooftop wall directly over where Leo had ascertained Bastion was now ensconced. Lowering their snake camera and audio equipment over the side, they expertly maneuvered it to the very top of the lighted window, checking the angles for maximum visual and auditory intel gathering.

Bastion sat at a large solid wood desk in an opulent office. Plush red carpet on the floor. Dark wood paneling on the walls. Built-in bookcases. A wide screen on one wall in the center filled with security camera video images from the casino's first floor. Leo remained quiet but had no doubt that Bastion kept an eye on the women coming through.

From what Natalie had said, it would not have been hard for him to have noted the movie crew that came in en masse and spied Carlotta Caruso. While she wasn't a superstar, from what Natalie had reported, Carlotta had diva tendencies that could have made someone think she was a bigger star than she was. *And maybe worth kidnapping.* And when he realizes his goons have taken the wrong woman, he had no doubt they would pay the ultimate price. *Now, if we can just find out where they took Abril before he realizes he has the wrong woman... if they did take the wrong woman.* They had no proof he didn't want Abril all along.

For almost thirty minutes, Bastion looked over paperwork, signing various documents and handing them to one of the men who'd come in with him. Whispering into his radio, Leo said, "There's a paper trail of his business but nothing electronic."

Carson was now the one who replied. "Old-fashioned, but it means someone has to have those pieces of paper to know what's going on. Even with government and police protection, he doesn't trust that someone wouldn't tap into his email or business records."

A knock on Bastion's office door drew Leo's focus, and they watched as the outside guard let in another man. Leo heard Natalie gasp into the radio, but she said nothing, and he wondered if she'd recognized the man entering the room. Sharing a glance with Rick, it was evident that he'd heard Natalie's slight sound and assumed the same thing.

Bastion looked up from his desk and smiled. "Is everything as planned? You have her?"

"Yes, Mr. Trejo. There were no problems getting her or transporting her."

"Has she been delivered to my estate in Puerto Champerico?"

"Yes, sir. I just returned from there after taking her myself."

Bastion nodded, then his eyes narrowed. "She was treated well? My instructions were followed?"

"Yes, sir. Your instructions were followed exactly. Other than being restrained, she was not harmed in any way. Instructions were given to the guard and the housekeeper there." The man rubbed his chin, allowing his lips to curve upward on one side. "Is she for Dante Herrera, sir?"

Bastion leaped from his seat, his fists landing on top of his desk. "That pig! No, she is not. She is mine. She'll bend to *my* will."

The man blinked, his head rapidly nodding as he swallowed audibly. "Yes, sir. I'm sorry, sir."

Bastion and the man stared at each other for a long moment, and Leo wondered if the man would be executed on the spot. Finally, the tension in Bastion's shoulders eased, and he slowly lowered himself back into his chair. "Keep her there. I want eyes on her. Keep her safe. Keep her comfortable. And no one, I repeat… no one touches her."

"Yes, yes, sir," the man agreed, bobbing his head again, glancing toward the two men still sitting on the sofa. "I'll see to it myself." The man backed toward the door, lowering his eyes. Feeling behind him for the doorknob, he pulled it open and hastened through, closing the door behind him.

Bastion then looked toward the two men still in the

room with him. "I'll leave tomorrow morning for my estate. Have the car ready for me by ten o'clock."

The two men nodded, then walked over to Bastion's desk. After picking up the files of signed paperwork, they placed them inside a briefcase before walking to the door. As one threw it open, giggles from the hallway could be heard. The guard outside escorted two scantily clad women teetering on sky-high heels inside the room. The guard closed the door, leaving Bastion alone with the women. He rounded his desk, undoing his tie, the gesture sending both women into a flurry of seeing who could disrobe him first.

Not wishing to see anymore, and sure as fuck not wanting Natalie to view what was going on, he and Rick pulled the camera up, rolling the tube and tucking everything away.

Alarico's voice came over the radio. "Can you get to the two men who have the briefcase? The evidence inside that Bastion signed would be invaluable to me."

Leo hesitated for a second, catching Rick's inquiring gaze. It would be no problem for the two of them to take care of the men and obtain the files from the brief-case, but to do so could jeopardize their mission of getting to Abril.

"No," Carson cut in, his voice definitive. "That's not our mission."

With their boss's words, he and Rick moved over to the side of the roof with the fire escape stairs. It appeared the casino kitchen staff was taking a break, so they waited in silence until the coast was clear before descending.

———

"Are you fuckin' nuts?" Natalie growled, unheeding the earpiece in her ear.

Alarico turned around, his eyes wide. "I told you, Ms. Robinson, that anything you could find needed to be turned over to me."

"Yes, *if* we find something in the course of getting to Abril, sure. But don't forget that her rescue is our primary mission. Is that in any way unclear to you?"

He stepped closer, his eyes glittering. "Your emotion is getting in the way of your objectivity."

Rearing back, she narrowed her eyes. "My emotion? Your lack of empathy for the person we're trying to save is getting in the way of your mission focus." Cocking her head to the side, she observed him carefully, refusing to back down.

He stepped closer again, then glanced over her shoulder. Just as she was about to move away, he leaped forward, moving faster than she expected. He clamped his hand around her mouth as he threw her to the ground, rolling her body under his, effectively pinning her in place. The gravel dug into her back. Unable to get loose, she shifted unsuccessfully to flip him. Pissed that she allowed him to take her down, she tried to bite his fingers.

He put his mouth close to her ear and said, "Be still. Someone's nearby."

She glanced up and saw his earpiece radio was still in place, which meant the Keepers, Leo, and Rick were listening. Steadying her breathing, she waited for either the danger to pass or for him to give her the opportunity to retaliate if he was lying. Suddenly, voices sounded nearby, and she remained quiet. After the voices grew softer and the footsteps moved away into the distance, he loosened his grip and assisted her up.

"I'm sorry," he began. "I didn't—"

Suddenly Leo appeared, his face like thunder, and he wrapped his hand around Alarico's throat. Rick stepped up to put his hand on the shoulder. "Bro, stand down."

Leo didn't flinch, but he looked toward Natalie. "You okay?"

She dipped her head up and down, sending her gaze to the three men. "It's okay, Leo. We were having a discussion, and I didn't realize someone was close by. Alarico's actions were surprising but necessary to keep our position from being revealed."

Leo released his grip, then stepped back, and she let out a sigh of relief. Feeling the need to defuse the situation, she stepped between Leo and Alarico, whose face was still red. Looking up at him, she tamped down her still-hot fuming. "I maintain that your end goal and ours are not the same, making it difficult for me to see how we can help each other. You're here to take down Bastion, and we're here for Abril. But I trust Carson and LSI-WC, so I'll keep my opinions to myself from now on."

She watched as the tension eased from his face, and he nodded.

"Thank you, Ms. Robinson, and I also apologize. In my line of work, getting my hands on anything that moves the cause further along is difficult. Because of that, my intention was good, but my timing was not."

"Well, if we're all friends again, I suggest we get the fuck outta here," Rick said, moving forward. "We've got to get to the coast."

Over the radio, Hop's voice was heard. "Already on it. Get back to the plane, and I can get you to another small airstrip that isn't cartel used and won't leave you too far to drive to get to his estate."

As they climbed back into the vehicle, she sucked in a deep breath and let it out slowly. Her adrenaline had spiked, but she knew they had a long night ahead. With Rick's and Alarico's attention out the windshield, she rested her hand on the seat between her and Leo, hoping he'd take her silent invitation. When his fingers wrapped around hers, she felt the warmth move through her body. Just his touch helped to recenter and refocus her wildly divergent thoughts. Looking toward him, she said, "At least we know where Abril is and that she's still alive and will be taken care of until we get to her."

Leo nodded, then offered a small smile as his reply, and her heart squeezed, skipping a beat.

18

The drive to the airport was filled with planning. Jeb had sent the floor plan and real estate agent pictures of the estate Bastion had bought just two years prior. For added backup, Dolby and Poole, who'd already flown into Mexico, had now taken charge of a boat on loan to the Keepers from a contact of Carson's. They were on their way to anchor offshore near the estate, ready to assist on land or provide a water getaway if the group was unable to get back to Hop at the airfield after the rescue.

Leo looked over at Natalie, whose gaze had not left her tablet as she studied the estate's layout. On the one hand, he was relieved for her assistance, considering her mission intel analysis was unparalleled. On the other hand, he wanted to rip the tablet from her hand and tell her not to worry about anything because he'd take care of it.

Squinting his eyes shut for a moment, he wondered where those thoughts were coming from. She'd been part of his mission support team, working behind the scenes with him for years. He acknowledged she'd handled her bodyguard duties with no problem. *Hell, I'm the one who wants her to come work for Carson with me. So why the fuck does it feel different now?*

Opening his eyes, his gaze skimmed over her furrowed brow as she bent over the tablet, and he longed to rub his finger over her skin. He had discovered her figure-hugging black shirt and jeans-covered curves in intimate detail. Yep, his best friend owned him lock, stock, and barrel. *And that's the difference.* He'd always loved her but now recognized that he was in love with her. And the desire to protect her battled all other thoughts.

"The place is a fucking open nightmare," Natalie bit out, her voice hard.

He turned toward her, but Jeb was already agreeing. "Yeah, I noticed that. The architecture isn't like what we're used to."

Leo had studied the outside, looking at the security measures, and hadn't looked at the floor plan yet. Turning to Natalie, he said, "Break it down for me."

"The main house. Colonial style that, believe it or not, was built in 1607, and modernized through the years. Ten bedrooms. Ten bathrooms. Three-car garage. Maids quarters. Almost ten-thousand square feet. All on one level, but it has two cupulas—"

"A cup of what?" Rick asked, twisting his neck around to look at her.

"A *cupula*," she repeated. "A small dome over the dining room and another one over... well, it could be the living area or the library. I can't tell what it's made of… just wood, plaster, or maybe some glass."

Without skipping a beat, she continued. "Tile and wood floors. We can hope they have some rugs to reduce sound, but the only photos I have to go off are from the last real estate listing when he bought it. The listing said that it came furnished. Probably the former owners were older and just wanted to get rid of everything. And with the high-end furniture I'm looking at, he probably kept it the same with some minor changes. Now, this is what you really need to know. There is a large courtyard in the middle surrounded by Spanish corridors. The bedrooms, living room, and dining room are all accessed from the open corridors. In other words, you don't have halls to traverse. Everything is accessible from the courtyard, and on the inside, one room just leads to another. This can be good or shitty, depending on who else is around, because there isn't a lot of privacy for slipping in. The kitchen is located off the dining room and courtyard, as well as the service quarters and garage. A large terrace at the back of the property overlooks the water."

"Does he have a separate office?" Alarico asked.

"There's no way to be sure. There is an open library on the other side of the living room from the dining room. Once he moved in, he could have added doors to separate this space off."

"Guard quarters?" Rick asked.

She sucked in a deep breath, then let it out slowly. "Hard to say. From the satellite pics that Jeb sent, I'd say he's added the building located at the side near the garage to the south. Large enough to house men who provide services for him, but until we get eyes on the place, I can't say for sure. I can't imagine he won't have some guards, even if it's not heavily fortified."

"So what are you thinking, Nat?" Leo asked. He knew they were all patched into LSI-WC, and they would all hear her ability to fine-tune the logistics of a mission.

She glanced up at him, her gaze roving over his face, settling on his eyes before looking back at the tablet. It struck him how often she had done that over the years when they worked together. Not hesitating, but simply sharing a look. And it also struck him how often she'd held his attention when she was planning over the years. She showed no hesitation in reporting to all with LSI-WC listening in. It ran through his mind that perhaps he should have already talked to her about working for Carson, but there was no time now. Sink or swim, this was her time to shine, and he knew she wouldn't fail them.

"If Jeb can patch into satellite views so we know where the guards are, we can use that information once we get closer to determine a point of entry. This late at night, the housekeeper might have already retired to her quarters, but we can keep an eye on her entrance. There are four bedrooms on one side, including the master. Bastion isn't married and, according to Alarico, doesn't have family nearby, so the three closer bedrooms could be where they possibly have Abril. There are six other bedrooms on the other side of the courtyard. Whether they are empty or used for some of his higher-ranking guards, employees, or friends, hopefully, Jeb's satellite views will help us determine that. But they only have windows facing the courtyard."

"What are your thoughts about the bedrooms straight off the courtyard?" Carson asked over the radio.

"Unlike a house with long winding halls hidden from satellite view, people will have to go through the courtyard to get to their bedrooms, the kitchen, or the living area. That means they're visible. The bedrooms nearest the main house have outside windows, so Rick and Leo can move around the outer perimeter of the house to check into the bedrooms before risking being seen inside the courtyard."

"Fuckin' perfect," Jeb said. "On it."

"Hang on," she warned. "Many of the outside windows have bars on them. Architectural bars for looks probably, but that doesn't mean they aren't functional for keeping people in or out, as well. So you can peer inside but may not be able to get through from the outside. The courtyard will still be the most accessible, although the most visible."

"What about the roof? Is it accessible?" Leo asked.

Her nose scrunched. "Maybe, but the building materials would be wood or stucco. Flat, so no attic. There is a rooftop patio with space for chairs and tables, but the access point is stairs on the side that leads down near the kitchen and garage. Chances are, it won't have any access to the rooms below."

"Except for the cup-o-la," Rick threw out with a wink.

Natalie didn't chuckle. Instead, her brow scrunched again as she peered back at her tablet. "You might be right... if they are anywhere near the dining room, his office would probably be located in that area. Especially if it has any glass, which would afford more accessibility if you needed an entrance point. At the very least, the structure would be old and possibly good for auditory surveillance."

"Good job, Natalie," Carson said.

Leo watched as a smile curved her lips, and his chest filled with pride. Looking back up toward Rick and Alarico, he said, "In the time it takes Hop to get us close, we'll have Jeb's information."

"And right on time," Rick called out, inclining his head out the front windshield toward the barely lit, dirt airstrip where Hop was waiting.

As Rick parked, they climbed from the SUV, grabbed their bags and equipment, and hurried toward the small plane.

Hop greeted them with a grin, then turned toward Natalie with his hand stretched forward. Shaking her hand, Hop's gaze moved from her up to Leo's face and back again, his grin still wide. "Natalie. Good to see you safe, and it sounds like we're lucky as fuck to have you working with us on this."

"I'm the grateful one, Hop. After all, I'm the one who landed with both feet in this mess and had to call upon you all."

"Not your fault," Hop assured. "Always keep the blame on the person who deserves it, and in this case, it's Bastion Trejo."

Noting her hand was still resting in Hop's, Leo stepped forward and hooked his arm around her shoulders, grumbling, "No time for small talk. Let's get into the air."

Hop and Rick burst out laughing, but they all followed Leo's lead and climbed aboard the small plane.

As soon as they were in the air, she turned toward Leo and leaned closer. "How is it that you guys can always have a plane or a vehicle no matter where you are?"

Leo didn't hesitate to give her the answer, something he never would've told any other civilian outside of LSI-WC. "Carson used to run CIA special ops. Between him and Mace Hanover of the original LSI in Maine, they use every available contact they can. They can pretty much get what we need in just about every country we might be in."

Nodding, she grinned. "Damn impressive. Sure as fuck puts my bodyguard job to shame!"

Alarico glanced over his shoulder at him, then slid his gaze to Natalie. "I have a question for you. What makes you think the bedrooms near Bastion's owner's suite will be empty?"

Without skipping a beat, she replied, "Human nature. It's a guess but one based on personality. Bastion has risen to the top by being smart, careful of who he trusts, and ruthless. He keeps his eyes and ears open for opportunities to serve the cartel, therefore serving himself. But we never see him with a lot of people around. Sure, he walks through the casino with a big smile and shakes the hands of many, but I only saw him with the two men, the same two we observed in his office. According to you, he's never seen with the same woman twice, so no long-term mistress. So even with the two men in his innermost circle, I doubt he wants to share a close sleeping arrangement with them."

She sucked in a deep breath and let it out slowly, appearing to give great consideration to her words before continuing. "Of course, it's pure supposition. There's a possibility that two of the bedrooms nearest him are occupied by those two closest guards, leaving another bedroom for a relative, a woman, or visitor." Suddenly shaking her head, she amended, "No. Since he doesn't have a committed relationship with a mistress, I can't imagine he'd want a one-night stand to have a bedroom close to his. So either the bedrooms are occupied by his closest associates or they're empty."

The men in the plane didn't speak, and as Leo also listened to the silence over the radio, he realized the same thing was happening at LSI-WC. "I think everything you said makes perfect sense, Nat," he said, nodding his head.

As the others nodded their agreement, she focused her gaze on him, and they shared a smile. Nothing about this woman should surprise him, considering he knew every expression, every mood, and had seen her at work over and over. Yet hearing her now helping to plan this mission and then his basking in the smile she bestowed, he was honored. And now that they'd finally given in to the desires that matched the feelings they shared, he had to battle to keep from getting hard, wanting nothing more than to pull her onto his lap and kiss her senseless.

"Almost here."

At Hop's words, Leo's attention was drawn out the window and down, seeing another strip of tiny lights barely indicating an airstrip below. With complete confidence in Hop's ability to land in the middle of the night on any kind of runway, he turned his mind back to the mission and hoped Jeb had a satellite view that they needed to either give credence or refute Natalie's assessment of where they could enter Bastion's estate to find Abril.

Ten minutes later, they were on the ground with an older car sitting to the side, ready for them. Hop walked over and said, "Poole and Dolby are in place, anchored about half a mile offshore. We're here for whatever you need. If you get out by the water, I'll be here to get Abril and Alarico back to Guatemala City or wherever they need to go."

Climbing into the back seat again with Natalie, Leo watched the dark shadows of night quickly swallow the airfield as Rick drove them down the narrow dirt road.

"ETA?" he asked.

"Jeb has sent the GPS coordinates for us to park at the edge of the jungle near the bottom of the small, inactive volcano," Rick said. "We'll cross by land, taking half an hour to get to the backside of the estate."

Leo turned to Natalie. "We'll stay in contact with you and—"

"Fuck that! I'm going in with you."

His brows darted downward. "The hell you are—"

"Shut the fuck up, you two, and listen," Rick cut in. "Jeb's got more intel."

"Natalie hit the nail on the head," Jeb confirmed. "I just looked at the satellite view and also discovered Bastion's home security on this estate is not as effective as at the casino or his older residence inland. You would think he'd want all his residences to be equally secure."

Alarico jumped in. "It's because he thinks he's invincible on his own turf. No one would dare do anything to him."

"The bedrooms near his?" Natalie prodded.

Leo grinned, knowing she lived for this shit and was fuckin' good at it.

"It appears all the activity is centered on the six bedrooms away from his," Jeb continued. "And the building that she assumed housed the guards. Other than the housekeeper, and one other man, I don't see historical evidence that anybody's using those main house bedrooms. But, we're in luck—"

"Abril!" Natalie all but shouted, her hand jerking out to clutch Leo's arm.

No longer caring if Rick or Alarico could spy his movements, he placed his hand over hers and squeezed. His gaze roved over her face as she stared at him, her eyes bright even in the minuscule light coming from the dashboard.

"Tapping into his security, which I have to admit is patchy and somewhat blurry, I was able to go back several hours and see a man accompany a woman to the area near Bastion's owner's suite. The angle was not good, and I can't see which room she may have gone into, but evidence supports that it could be Abril. The man had her by the upper arm, and while the woman was not restrained, she appeared to stumble occasionally."

"I wonder if she was drugged?" Leo surmised aloud, then felt Natalie's grip on his arm tighten. Turning toward her, he waited till he had her gaze pinned on him. "We'll get her. Now that we know more on how to get in and where she's being held, we'll get her."

"But I can help, Leo. There's no reason for me to stay outside."

"Natalie." Carson's voice over the radio had the power to halt any argument, instantly obtaining all Keepers' attention.

"Yes, sir?"

"I get how hard this is for you. But we all have our strengths, which makes us successful. You've just proven your worth with your analysis and intuition. But right now, we need you on the outside to continue to monitor the situation and offer that same level of analysis estimation moving forward. Leo and Rick are equipped and suited for the rescue mission."

Leo's breath halted in his lungs as he waited to see what Natalie would say. She could be hot-headed and argumentative, flippant and dismissive. But she also knew how to follow orders, and he waited to see which Natalie would respond to Carson.

"I understand, Carson," she said, her brow furrowed as she glanced toward Leo.

He let out a breath, realizing he never should've worried. This was his Natalie, worthy of being a Keeper.

19

Leo crept through the trees that led by the side of the estate, moving toward the water. With night vision goggles, he could maneuver through the thick under-growth of the tropical rainforest, noting the vegetation thinned as they moved away from the inland base of the volcano and came closer to the shoreline where the estate lay.

Rick was just in front of him, and Natalie was right behind. He'd never planned on having her in the thick of things, but she'd managed to change his mind. Why the fuck he'd been surprised, he had no idea. *I'd give her anything if I could.*

As he had been at the back of the vehicle strapping on equipment, she'd moved closer. Placing her hand on his arm, she'd indicated she wanted his attention, but the gesture wasn't necessary. He was always hyper aware of her, feeling her closeness even when they didn't touch. *Has it always been that way?* He couldn't remember the moment when she'd become the person he'd rather spend time with than anyone else. It just happened naturally.

"Leo," she'd whispered. "I want to get closer to the estate. Not to get in the way or hinder what you're doing, but closer."

He'd wondered what Carson thought of her words, then realized she'd slipped the radio from her ear and held it in her hand. Lifting a brow, he'd inclined his head toward her, almost laughing as she'd rolled her eyes and made a face.

"First, if I'm closer and you need help with Abril, she'll trust me. Also, I still have a strange feeling about Alarico." With that, she'd cut her eyes to the side, and Leo had followed her gaze, staring at the other man tapping into his phone. Looking back at Natalie, he'd waited.

"I know he kept me from being discovered earlier when we were outside the casino, but I wasn't paying attention because he and I were arguing. He wants the information to take down Bastion. I get that, but I think he'll try to get inside to get his hands on anything he can to meet his end goal. And his end goal has nothing to do with Abril's rescue."

Not willing to go off the grid, he'd inclined his head toward the radio in her hand again, and she'd narrowed her eyes at him before slipping the earpiece back into place. Changing the frequency to one Carson would realize was just for him, he'd stepped to the side and succinctly repeated Natalie's concerns without allowing Alarico to listen in.

Rick had stared at them from over the top of the

vehicle, unable to hear what was being said, but accepted his silent assurance with a chin lift and went back to suiting up.

"I agree that Natalie can accompany you part of the way," Carson acknowledged. "Natalie, I know I shouldn't have to say this, considering your background, but you don't fall under my employee orders. But for this mission to succeed, you've got to see it that way. Get to where you can watch the courtyard. You can radio to Leo and Rick if there is any activity that we can't see on the security."

"Absolutely, Carson," she'd agreed, then looked up at Leo and grinned.

And just like always, he'd smiled in return. Going back to their original frequency, Carson announced, "Natalie will accompany Rick and Leo just to the edge of the estate. If new intel needs to be analyzed on-site, she'll be there to do it and help with Abril."

Rick had grinned widely, but Alarico's gaze darted around the others, his expression hard but remained quiet. Leo handed her a gun and watched with satisfaction as she checked the ammunition and safety before jamming it into the back of her waistband.

"Let's go," Leo had said after a few seconds of hesitation, falling in line behind Rick.

Approaching the low wall on the north side, they stopped. Twisting around toward Natalie, he reminded her, "Watch the courtyard. If there's any problem, get down to the beach, and you'll be picked up. One of them will be onshore as our backup if we need them."

"Got it," she agreed.

He glanced toward Alarico, then hesitated. He and Rick had their own mission but had no idea what Alarico might do that would help or hinder them. "Keep in mind what we're here to do," he warned, holding the other man's gaze. Alarico's jaw tightened, but he offered a short nod.

He looked over his shoulder, a multitude of emotions tied up in the intensity of his lingering gaze on her. Dark hair pulled back. Face pale in the moonlight. So fuckin' familiar. So fuckin' beautiful.

She stared back and then winked. As always with her, he could barely keep a smile off his face. With a chin lift, he moved forward with Rick.

From what he could see as they circled around the outer perimeter of the estate, Jeb was right, and Bastion's security was light. There were no roaming guards, but as they slipped toward the back of the property, they observed a few men sitting on a picnic table outside the building they'd identified as possible guard quarters. Chatting, smoking, walking around. Only two had gun holsters strapped over their shoulders, but their stances gave evidence they expected no threat. The building was not large, indicating Bastion's on-estate forces were probably less than a dozen.

No high wall surrounded the estate like many drug lords who lived in prosperity and seclusion. Bastion's estate could've been owned by any legitimate businessman with minimal worry that someone might come in. Alarico had probably been right on that score— Bastion didn't fear anyone making an attempt on him. He had the backing of the cartels and the protection of some government officials and some in law enforcement. He was a man who came and went, seemingly unable to be touched.

As they noted the position of the guard quarters, he changed the frequency again, blocking everyone other than LSI-WC. Keeping his voice low, he said, "Check Alarico's phone. He was sending a message to someone as we were getting ready to leave. I know he's supposed to have men watching the casino to see when Bastion leaves, but I want to know."

As much as Carson had said he trusted the man who gave him Alarico's name and information, Leo knew Carson would not be offended at them running extra checks. In their business, continually sifting through all intel made them safe and the best.

"He sent a message to another detective in his office," Chris replied. "He asked them about Bastion's movements."

"Any reply?"

"Not in text."

"According to Carson's contact, Alarico has people in his department who he trusts. Those who haven't been bought by the cartel."

Flipping back to the original channel, he kept his thoughts to himself. Natalie had voiced her concerns, and he took them seriously. But right now, his goal was to get to Abril and keep an eye on Alarico to make sure nothing he did harmed their chances of getting the young woman out safely. Anything else the detective accomplished was up to him.

Coming to the edge of the trees surrounding the

property, he spied the large rocks creating a barrier leading to the sandy shore below. Glancing out toward the ocean's dark waters, he knew that Dolby and Poole were anchored just offshore, ready to come to Bastion's dock if needed. Leo and Rick moved out together, staying in the shadows and effortlessly gliding between the thick vegetation as they made their way over the low garden wall in the back. The estate was mostly cloaked in darkness, with few lights in the separate bedroom areas.

He'd looked at the main house when Natalie had been examining it. The one-story stucco structure was unremarkable from the outside, but he had no doubt it was impressive on the inside. After reading about Bastion and hearing Natalie's description, he bet the man liked to live large.

Jeb had been watching the security, reporting that the housekeeper had only gone into two of the six extra bedrooms on one side of the estate earlier that day, indicating the others were empty. On the owner's side, no one had been seen leaving, indicating that the man and woman entering earlier were still there, although Jeb warned them that he did not have full visibility of the bedroom doors sheltered by the covered walkway.

He and Rick hastened to the side of the stucco-sided main house, stopping near the outer bedroom windows close to the owner's suite. The bars were decorative, but it would take time to remove them and could possibly alert the few guards at the back.

Using their snake camera, they scanned the inside and quickly determined the first bedroom was unoccupied. Slipping to the next window, they observed a suited man sitting on a settee in the bedroom, watching a game on the flatscreen television mounted on the wall.

"He's alone," Rick whispered. "But there's no window in the bathroom."

"Check the next one before we take him out," Leo responded. He glanced to the side as Rick hustled over, maneuvered his snake camera to the corner of the window, and then shook his head. Leo nodded. "She could be in the bathroom. Or in Bastion's bedroom if she's on this side of the estate, but I swear, I can't see this guy taking a chance of her escaping."

Hop, stationed at the end of the road leading into the estate, reported, "Large SUV just passed. Possibly Bastion inside, but I can't tell."

Shit. "If it is, then he left the casino earlier than he planned," Leo growled. Knowing they only had about ten minutes before someone else arrived, he wondered if it was Bastion and why Alarico's contact didn't let them know. *Unless they let him know, and he kept it to himself.*

"Housekeeper just came from the kitchen," Natalie radioed. "Heading toward the bedroom two doors down from Bastion's."

Turning his attention back to the snake camera, he observed the door open and watched as the housekeeper walked in with a cup of coffee in her hand. Offering it to the man, he accepted and murmured his thanks. She turned and started toward the door, speaking again. Leo's Spanish was passable, but he was glad Andrew was on the other end of LSI-WC for translating to make sure he wasn't missing anything.

"She said Mr. Trejo is on his way home and wanted the woman ready to be taken to his study when he called for her."

"She's now heading to the courtyard," Leo said, receiving Rick's tight-jawed nod. To get to Abril, they needed to take the guard out faster than they had hoped and had lost the advantage of Bastion not coming until the morning.

"I thought Alarico had someone watching the casino to let us know when Bastion was leaving." Leo made the statement over the radio, knowing full well that the detective was listening.

"My contact gave no signal he had left," Alarico radioed, his tone biting.

Leo caught Rick's grimace and knew he had the same expression on his own face. *Natalie's instincts and suspicions may be proved right.* Remaining quiet, they slipped through the vegetation along the outer walls toward the back of the estate, getting into position to scale the low brick wall leading to the courtyard and away from the guard quarters.

"Vehicle pulling into second garage space," Jeb said. "No visual inside the garage, so I won't be able to see who it is."

"I'll see them when they enter the courtyard," Natalie assured.

Leo and Rick halted just outside the short wall waiting for her intel. His focus was on point, although memories flooded of countless missions where he'd relied on Natalie's voice over the radio as she kept abreast of the ever-changing intel of missions. Back then, just hearing her kept him grounded. Now, having her work with him again filled him with a sense of rightness.

"Shit, it's Bastion," she announced over the radio. "He's heading straight to the main section of the house, not his bedroom. Two men are with him, but they are veering toward the far bedrooms on the other side of the courtyard. He must be going to the dining room or his office."

"I'm going in," Rick said. "I can take those two from there."

Leo nodded and was about to move into the courtyard as well when Natalie spoke again.

"The housekeeper has just come out of her room again, now with two cups of coffee, and she's walking over to the two men."

Leo silently cursed, thinking the older woman would be in bed and sound asleep by this time. They didn't want her to get spooked and set off any alarm to warn Bastion they were here.

A tense moment passed. "Okay, she's handed cups to the two men who came in with Bastion and finished talking. She's returning to her quarters, and the two men have disappeared into two different bedrooms. The last one on each end, leaving four empty rooms between them."

Finally, a piece of luck. Leo shot a victorious look toward Rick, receiving his nod in return. Bastion may have given his top henchmen the rooms far apart with the idea that they would be more effective covering a wider area of the inner courtyard, but separated by so much space would make taking them out much easier.

Slipping over the last short wall into the courtyard, Leo stayed in the shadows as he moved along, knowing Rick would do the same. The middle of the courtyard was covered in neatly mowed grass, but the perimeter was lush with massive potted plants, palm trees, and ferns as tall as he. Following Natalie's intel, he and Rick reconned the area and then sent hand signals as they each chose a different room. With a snake camera at the front window, Leo could see his target moving into the bathroom, his weapon unholstered and lying on the table next to the bed. *Fuckin' easy.*

Signaling again to Rick, he moved in, finding the door unlocked. *A fuckin' idiot, as well.* It only took a few seconds for him to come up behind the man as he was bent over the sink with running water, take him in a carotid restraint hold, and render the man unconscious. Zip-tying his wrists behind him and his ankles, he gagged the man before hastening back into the bedroom and snagged the exposed weapon.

By the time he reached the doorway, Rick was just exiting the other man's room. Leo didn't have to ask to know that the other Keeper had been as successful as he with neutralizing both of Bastion's commanders.

"Maid has gone into her quarters," Natalie reported. "Her light is still on."

Considering the poor lighting and sketchy security cameras in the area, hampering Jeb's ability to monitor and radio everyone's locations, Leo appreciated Natalie forcing her way into the active mission. Signaling Rick again, they moved back into the lush vegetation surrounding the perimeter of the courtyard heading toward the main living area.

He glanced toward the bedroom door where the man sat, waiting for further instructions from Bastion before bringing the woman to him. Leo was still uncertain if Abril was inside but hoped the woman they had referenced was her.

"Going in?" Rick asked.

Nodding, he started to move forward, but Natalie's voice halted his steps. Hearing her words over the radio, he jerked his wide-eyed gaze toward Rick, seeing the same expression on his fellow Keeper's face.

20

"Alarico! Where are you going? Stop!"

Natalie, still crouched behind a small wall that had given her optimum visuals of the courtyard, had startled when Alarico darted past her. He didn't respond, which pissed her off even more. While keeping an eye on the ever-changing situation unfolding in front of her, needing to accurately report what was happening so Leo and Rick would be safe as they found and rescued Abril, she hadn't paid attention to Alarico's whereabouts.

But now, as he brushed against her shoulder when he darted past, she watched as he bent and followed the low wall leading toward the tiled patio between the garages and the kitchen. As he came to the end, he crawled over the wall and circled toward the stairs leading to the rooftop patio.

"Fuck," she murmured, torn between following him and staying where she was.

"Sit-rep," came the order through the radio, jerking

her back to those who were listening.

"Alarico has left his position and is moving toward the garage."

"Alarico?" Carson called over the radio, but no response was forthcoming. "If you hear me, report." Still, no response.

With Leo and Rick in position to handle the man left guarding Abril, she looked around for a few seconds in indecision. *Shit!* The Delta missions she worked on had everyone doing exactly what they were trained to do... and no rogue decisions were made that lessened the team's effectiveness. In fact, every decision by every team member was made to further the mission and work in unison. *What the fuck is he doing?*

"Dammit," she muttered aloud, deciding to follow Alarico. Whatever he was doing, she needed to let the others know. "Following," she radioed. No one spoke, but she had no doubt that they were angry. *Hopefully, just with him and not me.* But Leo's safety, as well as Rick's and Abril's were first on her mind. All other considerations took a back seat.

Continuing to crouch low, she followed Alarico's path along the wall toward the garage, her head swinging side to side to ascertain she was not observed. As she came to the end, she carefully looked around toward the tall stucco wall that contained the stairs leading to the rooftop patio. Grimacing, she slipped along the shadows of the garage and peered around the bottom of the stairs. Seeing Alarico disappear at the top, she was filled with rage. "He's ascended the outer stairs to the rooftop," she reported. "Following."

Body vibrating with adrenaline, she glanced behind her and darted up the steps when she didn't see anyone. At the top, she spied him moving along the edge, peering over the sides. Coming up behind him, she grabbed his arm, ducking when he whirled around with his fist out.

"What are you doing?" she whispered, pinning him to the tile with her narrow-eyed glare.

"I've got my own mission," he whispered in return, his dark eyes glaring but his fingers loosening. "You take care of yourself and leave me to my business."

Continuing to hold on to his arm, she gripped him tighter, knowing her size belied her strength. "You fuck things up for anyone I care about down there, and make no mistake, I'll fuck you over," she warned, her words like knife blades as they cut through the air between them.

His eyes widened for a second before he jerked his arm from her grasp. Without speaking again, he turned and moved over the next wall that separated the patio from the rest of the rooftop, crawling to the closest dome. Radioing his location, she followed once again. Whatever he was going to do, she wanted to be right there to witness and provide the necessary information to the others.

Climbing over the wall, she moved to crouch next to him, ignoring the glare he sent her way. Looking down, she realized part of the cupola was glass. While not perfectly clear, she could make out Bastion sitting at his desk, papers still spread before him. *That's what Alarico is still after... those damn papers.*

"At cupola over the library office. Glass pane allows visibility and some auditory. Bastion is located just below at desk," she whispered into the radio.

"Alarico?" Leo asked.

"Next to me."

She felt the detective's heated stare but ignored him. Looking down, she watched as Bastion collected the papers on his desk and replaced them in the folders. He made notations in a notebook, then closed it and wrapped a band to secure the pages. Tapping the files together to settle the papers in a stack, he placed the notebook on top, then stood and walked to a safe built into the bookcase. Once opened, he placed the folders inside. Alarico grumbled and shifted but remained in place.

Bastion moved back to his desk and pressed a button on an intercom. "Bring her in now."

"He's called for the woman," she whispered, alerting the others.

"Moving in," Leo responded.

"Fuck," Rick grunted. "The housekeeper is coming out of her room. Goddammit, she's the one escorting a woman."

The housekeeper had Abril in her room? Or is it some other woman? Fuck! Natalie's heart pounded as she imagined the way Leo would have to instantly recalculate how to get to Abril and take out the man still in the other bedroom without alerting Bastion.

"Housekeeper is close to the entrance of the main house," Leo said. After a moment, he added, "They are entering."

"I've got the man in the bedroom," Rick said. "You stay with the women."

Natalie bent lower to peer down through the glass, her heart squeezing when a movement from the far corner of the room caught her attention. The housekeeper walked in, her hand on the upper arm of a woman whose long, dark hair hung down, obscuring her face. Remembering Abril wore dark pants and a white, short-sleeved blouse when taken, the clothing appeared to match. *Look up... come on, look up.* While they would rescue any woman taken against her will, she desperately wanted it to be Abril.

Her breathing halted as she waited, then the woman below slowly lifted her head, exposing her tearstained face. *Abril!*

"You have visual?" Leo asked.

Not realizing she'd spoken aloud, she nodded before catching herself in the worthless motion. "Yes. It's her. In his office. The housekeeper is leaving—"

"Who the fuck is this?" came the roar from Bastion below, his fist hitting the top of his wooden desk with a bang.

Natalie jumped, as did Alarico next to her, and it was obvious that the housekeeper and Abril visibly startled as well. "He—"

"Heard him," Leo acknowledged. "Think everyone did."

Bastion turned to the housekeeper and ordered, "Get Ramirez. Now!" He reached into his top drawer and pulled out a gun.

The older woman's face creased in a frown, but she immediately turned and ran from the room.

"He's got a gun and sent her to get Ramirez." Natalie tried to keep the shakiness from her voice, finding it harder to report from the midst of the action rather than from the distance of the support team location.

Leo reported, "Housekeeper is coming out. Heading to the Ramirez room. Stand down, Rick. Moving closer."

She knew Rick had been slipping into the man's room to neutralize him and hoped Leo's words would stop him in time. Now that Bastion had discovered that the woman in his possession wasn't Carlotta, Abril was at more risk, especially with his weapon waving around as he stomped to the other side of his desk. "He's rounding the desk. His back is to the open doorway. His weapon isn't on her but in his hand."

"Ramirez heading toward the office. Housekeeper going into her room."

Just after Leo's report, another movement caught her eye, and she observed a man hurry into the room, straightening his tie. His worried gaze darted back and forth between Abril and Bastion. "Sir?"

"Who the fuck is this?" Bastion spoke, his voice hard, each word like granite, jerking his head and the gun toward Abril.

"Th...the woman... the woman you wanted."

"This is not the woman I told you to get!"

"But... you said she was on the street... the one you saw in the casino—"

Natalie's gaze never left Abril's face as she stared

down at her friend, unable to do anything to help other than watch and pray that they could get to her without Bastion firing at Abril.

"Not this la puta. I wanted the American. The guard dog. The one whose eyes dared to look at me. The one who threatened me. She was to be mine. That is the bitch I want to bring to heel."

Natalie swallowed her gasp as she heard him say who he'd wanted to kidnap... not Abril. Not Carlotta. *Me!* Her chest heaved as the air left her lungs, barely hearing Leo's whispered, "Fuck."

Leo's softly spoken curse slid from his lips when hearing that Natalie was the intended kidnapping victim. *And not for ransom but just for this piece of shit.* He'd made it to the edge of the courtyard near the entrance to the dining room. He could see Abril but had no visual of Bastion from his position. But with the open doorway and connecting rooms, it was easy to hear the two men.

The underling's voice trembled. "Th... this was the one I saw... the one you said was on the street. I thought—"

Bastion growled, "You are not paid to think! This bitch was with her, but you let the one I wanted get away."

"I'm sorry, Mr. Trejo. I'll—"

"But nothing! The one I wanted is long gone, and you'll pay for that mistake."

Hop's voice cut through over the radio. "Incoming. Four vehicles. Unable to identify."

"Just got them on radar," Jeb added. "Already on the lane leading to your location."

"Stand down," Alarico interrupted over the radio. "They're my men."

Leo grit his teeth, knowing they were about to get caught in a battle between Alarico and Bastion's men. "A fuckin' gunfight at the O.K. Corral is not what we need."

He heard Carson radio to Alarico but focused on trying to get closer to Abril without being seen in the open corridors. "Need a diversion away from the main house."

"On it," Dolby called back. "Clear at back?"

"Clear," Rick reported. "Housekeeper neutralized."

"Clear." Leo felt a stab of relief knowing Dolby and Poole had more tricks up their sleeves than just anchoring offshore or hanging down on the dock.

Natalie cursed, "Shit... Alarico has left... he's going back down the stairs."

"Stay where you are," Leo ordered, wanting her out of the way of whatever Dolby planned and knowing her eyes on the situation below her were vital.

Within a few seconds, a small explosion was heard toward the back of the estate, beyond the guard quarters and near the rocks leading to the beach. Swinging his head to the side, he saw smoke rising, quickly followed by the crackling sounds of a fire at the edge of a wooden outbuilding.

Bastion roared at the sound, but Leo still couldn't see him from his position. Natalie immediately reported, "Weapon still on Abril, but he's looking around."

"Go, go!" Bastion yelled. "Get Matteo and Jose!"

Leo assumed he was ordering Ramirez to get the two men Bastion had arrived with. His assumption was confirmed as the man raced past Leo's concealed location, knowing Rick would take care of him. Waiting for Natalie's sign, she surprised him when she barked, "He's taking Abril through another door... behind a bookcase on the eastern side."

Leo grimaced as he crouched down, hastening through the dining room to follow. Entering the now-empty library, he whirled at a sound behind him, his weapon drawn. "Goddammit," he cursed, seeing Alarico running into the room. The detective moved to the desk, looked around wildly, then ran over to the wall safe.

"What the fuck are you doing?" Leo growled.

"I'm getting the evidence I came for," Alarico said, his face hard. "My men are on their way, and I can take him and those close to him down with these files."

"You fucker... you never planned on helping get Abril." Leo stood to his full height, glaring down at the man.

"I'm going after Abril," Natalie cried out over the radio, her words jolting Leo into action. Without another look backward, he darted toward the bookcase door that was still partially open and entered a narrow hallway that ran the length of the house, leading toward the back of the estate.

21

Natalie had no plan in mind, which was unusual for her, but then she'd always been with support in the safety of the background, never *boots on the ground* in the middle of an ongoing, active mission. Flying down the concrete steps, she could see that the driveway was now filled with several more SUVs, men with weapons piling from them and racing toward the guard quarters in the back. Within seconds, the sound of gunfire broke out. Leaping over a low wall, she crouched as she scuttled in a different direction toward the back of the estate, hoping that Bastion and Abril would have to come out somewhere on that side, away from the flames she could now see rising into the dark sky from the explosion she knew Dolby and Poole had created.

Creeping along with great caution, she spied a wooden door slam open in the side of the building up ahead, and Abril stumbled forward, crying out as Bastion's hand gripped her upper arm tightly. The gun was still in his other hand. Natalie ducked behind a large fern, her heart pounding as she assessed his position and her chances to take him down without Abril getting hurt. The area was brighter now that several security lights in the courtyard had been engaged, casting their illumination over the low wall. With the increased visibility, she could easily see that he was alone with Abril.

"I should kill you now, but you'll at least be worth something on the market," he growled to Abril, still pulling her along, sticking the barrel of his gun in her side.

"No, please—"

"Shut up!" He turned toward the flames on the other side of the estate and grimaced. "Go. We'll get to my boat."

Knowing Dolby and Poole were on the dock, Natalie prayed they wouldn't shoot at Bastion and possibly hit Abril. *I need to get to her first!*

"On the north side. Need backup," she whispered into her radio before plunging from the plant she had hidden behind.

Bastion was staring at the fire, but Abril caught sight of her almost immediately and gasped, drawing Bastion's attention.

His eyes widened a second before a smirk crossed his face, the gold tooth glinting in the now lit walkway. "Well, well... I guess the guard dog came for you after all." His fingers released Abril's arm, but he shoved her to the ground as he lifted his weapon toward Natalie.

She never dropped her gaze from his as she slowly knelt and wrapped her arms around a shaking Abril, who clutched her tightly. Still watching him, she whispered to Abril, "Are you okay?"

"You came." The hoarse whisper ended in a sob.

She nodded, wanting to look into Abril's face both to assure and for assurance but refused to give Bastion more of an advantage than he already had with his weapon on them. She forced her lips to curve upward in encouragement, squeezing her hand. "Of course I did." Helping Abril stand and ensure she was steady on her feet, she gently moved her to the side and stepped around to shield her friend's body with her own.

Keeping her hardened, unflinching gaze on Bastion, she was acutely aware of his weapon in her peripheral vision but didn't give him the satisfaction of acknowledging his upper hand. "You went to a lot of trouble for me. What's wrong? Can't get a woman on your own?"

His black eyes somehow darkened even more, but hot rage ran through Natalie's veins, giving her courage... or foolishness.

Carson's low voice came over her earpiece, caution dripping off her name. "Natalie."

She swallowed and re-centered, knowing that antagonizing Bastion wouldn't help get Abril to safety, especially not knowing if Leo or the other Keepers were close by or engaged in their own battles with the guards.

Bastion stepped closer, the barrel of his gun held straight toward her chest. "You talk too much, bitch. But you intrigued me. I considered taking you before you left my casino. But with the other Americans around, I decided you weren't worth the risk. But when I saw you on the street, I knew you were a chance I had to take. You were going to be mine. I knew it was fate."

She jerked slightly, then shook her head in disbelief. "Fate? You've got to be shitting me. My being there was nothing more than a coincidence. It sure as fuck wasn't fate."

He lifted a brow. "There are no coincidences in life. We make our own destiny out of what the gods give us. And your eyes defied me once. But to defy me again was too much to ignore."

"My eyes are still on you, asshole," she warned, fighting to keep the sneer off her face.

The gunfire came closer, and Abril flinched as she whimpered. It now sounded as though the police and Bastion's guards had taken their war into the courtyard. Bastion's smirk dropped slightly, and his gaze darted to the side. Her lips tightened at the idea that Leo and Rick would be in the firefight as well, but she trusted they could take care of themselves. Without taking her eyes off Bastion, she felt Abril's still shaking presence behind her.

He jerked the gun as he inclined his head. "Let's go."

"The beach? You want us to go to the beach?" Knowing the warning to Dolby and Poole would have them ready, she kept her face blank, realizing that Bastion had not divined that she had an earpiece radio.

"Shut up, bitch, and move." When she hesitated, he glared, waving his gun. "Or your Guatemalan look-alike dies right here."

Abril's breath hitched, infuriating Natalie even more. Reaching behind her, she snagged Abril's hand, giving it a squeeze and checking to feel that her weapon was hidden under her shirt. "Come on. Stick with me," she said softly, stepping forward and pulling Abril along with her. As Bastion let them pass so he could keep the gun trained on her, she moved Abril in front. "Stay on the path toward the beach," she said, knowing their location was radioed to the Keepers.

As Abril stumbled ahead, Natalie swung her gaze around, seeing little in the dark as they moved away from the lights in the courtyard. Hearing the sounds of the continued gunfire, she focused on the man behind her.

"Coming from behind you, Nat," Leo radioed. "Drop when I say."

Proceeding forward, she wondered how to get Abril out of the way. Reaching out as though to hold her again, Natalie kept moving, waiting for Leo's voice to come through her earpiece.

Shouting and the sounds of running came closer from the courtyard side. Gunfire ricocheted past, and she shoved Abril to the ground, throwing herself on top, squelching any screams Abril tried to emit. Assuming Leo was stuck in the midst of the battle between the police and the guards, she twisted her head and caught sight of Bastion, his head swinging all around, eyes wide. His gaze dropped to her, and he pointed his weapon right at her again as his eyes narrowed.

"Get up, or you both die now."

She obeyed, her jaw tight. "Leave her… take me. I'm the one you want."

He ducked as the sound of gunfire grew closer, then

snagged Natalie's arm, placing the barrel of the gun against her ribs. "Go, or I will kill her."

Looking down into Abril's terrified face, she ordered, "Stay here by the gate to the courtyard," giving their location to anyone listening over the radio.

Moving slowly, she crouched in front of Bastion and stumbled toward the path leading down to the beach. Hearing Abril scream, she whirled around in time to see Rick leap over the wall and land next to the frightened young woman.

"Friend of Natalie's," he called out, his arms wrapping around her. The air rushed from Natalie's lungs at the sight of him lifting her friend and then racing toward the front of the estate.

"Go!" Bastion yelled, spittle flying from his mouth as he grabbed Natalie's arm, still crouching as he pushed her.

"Fuck you!" she bit out, determined not to allow him to move her farther. Leo's voice came over the radio at the same time Bastion screamed at her. She thought she heard "Drop!" so she ducked to the ground, uncertain if that was the right thing to do. A large, dark shadow rushed from behind, but as Bastion turned toward the shadow, he fired, then a mass of tangled bodies hit the ground near her.

She scrambled to her knees, her gaze landing on Leo's face contorted with a grimace as he lay on his back, a hole in his shirt near the top of the body armor he wore. Her chest depressed as the air rushed from her lungs, and she flung herself to his side. "Shit, Leo," she growled, knowing that while the armor stopped the bullet from entering his body, the hit knocked him backward. Spinning around, she spied Alarico running toward them, his gun raised. "Augh!" she yelled, reaching back to grab the handle of her weapon. The rage she'd felt earlier was nothing compared to the eruption of adrenaline.

Alarico jumped to the top of the low wall, then readied to leap down to where they were as Bastion battled to regain his footing and lifted his weapon, training it on her.

"Shift, babe."

She looked down to see Leo's hand on his weapon, both hidden behind her body. With a nod, she fell to the side as both she and Leo aimed and fired at the same time. Bastion's body jerked wildly, then fell backward, a dark stain on his shirt growing as he hit the ground.

Two men raced up from the beach path with their weapons drawn. Grabbing Leo's weapon, she jumped to her feet but halted as they called out, "Dolby. Poole." Nodding, she said, "Help him." Both men hastened over to assist Leo to his feet.

Alarico cursed, his eyes wide as he stared down at Bastion's body. Looking up toward her, he snarled, "I wanted him alive. Alive! With him, I could take down so many more!"

Lifting her gun, she pointed it toward Alarico, taking pleasure in the gasp he emitted as his eyes widened, no longer caring about any cooperation between him and the Keepers. Her chest heaved with anger as she bit out, "I should fuckin' shoot you. Christ, give me one reason I shouldn't."

"Nat."

Her name slipped from Leo's mouth. That was all she heard. Just the one word. But the sound of her name coming from the man whose heart was synced with hers calmed her into rationality. A huff sounded as the air rushed from her lungs. Shaking her head slowly, she lowered her gun. "You're an asshole, but not worth the trouble of killing you right now."

The sounds of gunfire had stopped, and a quick glance over his shoulder showed the heavily armed police officers herding the few guards left alive. As she walked over to the detective, the raging inferno that had flowed through her morphed into a cold river in her blood. "You bastard. You fucking bastard. You were never here to assist with Abril. Your actions nearly cost her her life."

"To take down a man like Bastion Trejo, some have to be sacrificed, Ms. Robinson," he ground out. "Arresting him would force his hand to give up others. Even some in the police or government. He would have told me anything to make his charges go away."

She rocked back a step, gut-punched. "You... you were going to sacrifice all of us." As she stepped closer, her gaze never wavered from his eyes, barely noting his defiant, lifted chin. "I don't know who's worse... that piece of trash lying dead on the ground or you."

"I wouldn't expect a woman to understand," he sneered.

"Why you..."

"Babe," Leo grunted.

She turned to see him take a step toward her, and

the breath caught in her lungs as she stared at the man who held her heart. This man who'd fought for his country with a no-man-left-behind attitude. This man who'd shared years of laughter along with a few tears, pizza and beer, quiet nights, and noisy bars. This man who'd now declared his love for her, proving their friendship was just the basis for who they were becoming. And Alarico's actions could have gotten them killed before they'd had a chance to be together.

Swallowing deeply, she fought to drag in oxygen as her chest quivered. He lifted his arm and wiggled his fingers for her to take his hand, fighting against a wince of pain that crossed his face at the motion.

Shaking her head slightly, she turned from Leo and stalked the few steps to stand in front of Alarico, who had started shouting orders to his men.

He glared, his eyes narrowing as he dismissed her. "I don't have time to listen to you, Ms. Robinson. I've got a job to do."

"Yeah? Well, so do I." She cocked her arm, and before he could move, her fist swung out. Connecting with his face, she dropped him to the ground as his head snapped back.

"Damn," came the utterance from several of the men around, but she ignored them all as she turned and walked straight toward a now-grinning Leo. Moving underneath the arm on his uninjured side, she let out a long slow breath as he held her tight with one arm. She felt his lips as he kissed the top of her head and the tilting world stopped spinning, suddenly righting itself.

Just like all the times she watched him come in from a mission and knew he was safe.

"You guys ready to head home?" Dolby asked.

"I'm already home," she whispered. Right here. Right now. With this man. In his arms.

An hour later, Natalie stood in the drive, the pre-dawn light barely streaking the sky. The noise of gunfire and shouts had given way to birds waking up and filling the air with their chirps and squawks. She lifted her head and stared into the jungle, its nature-filled beauty so in contrast to the ugliness of the night. With the jungle leading to the forested volcano in the distance and the crystal-clear blue of the ocean behind, she sucked in a deep breath and then let it out slowly.

The estate had been swarmed by more Guatemalan first responders as ambulances had taken away the dead and injured. Alarico, who now sported a bruise on his left cheek and a black eye, organized his staff as they combed through the house, compiling the paper trail of evidence that Bastion had kept on his casino dealings and God-knows-what-else. From the smile on Alarico's face, she assumed he found what he needed to shut down the casino and arrest some of the higher-ups he wanted to get his hands on. She sucked in a deep breath, then let it out slowly. She didn't begrudge him for doing his job, nor did she have difficulty admitting his job was necessary. *But his methods? Fuck that.*

Carson had been apprised of the situation in its

entirety and was livid, making sure his contact who'd vouched for Alarico knew they would not expect any cooperation with LSI-WC in the future. A smile slipped across her face. Like her, Carson wanted successful missions, but first and foremost, he cared about his Keepers.

The sound of her name being called out had her turn just in time to steady her body as Abril rushed forward. She'd been interviewed by Alarico's men but had very little she could tell them. She'd been kept blindfolded and restrained until being brought to the estate and placed in the housekeeper's room.

The two women stood with their arms wrapped around each other, their dark eyes shining with tears.

"I still can't believe you came for me," Abril said, letting out a shaky breath. "I thought you would be back in America by now, and when they discovered that I was not you, then they'd kill me."

She knew if they had grabbed Abril after her taxi was farther away, that's exactly what would have happened. But she just smiled and said, "You're safe. And what's more, the people who took you are all dead. You'll be able to return to your life without worrying about looking over your shoulder all the time."

Abril nodded and glanced to the side before bringing her gaze back to her. "I like your friends. I especially like the one who can't take his eyes off you. He's the one you talked about, isn't he?"

A small snort erupted. "Yeah, he is. Best friend I've ever had."

"And more than friends, I think?"

Natalie leaned back and pursed her lips. "With as much drama as the last few days have brought for you, I'd think that wondering about my love life wouldn't be high on your priorities."

"Oh, no," Abril said, shaking her head. "When you almost lose your life, you realize what's important. And the way your friend keeps his eyes on you, I know you're important to him."

No quip came forth as Natalie nodded, feeling Abril's words deeply. "You're right. And yes, he's important to me, too."

They shared a heartfelt smile as the sun lifted a little more in the sky. "I will miss you and hope you will return to Guatemala someday. My country is so much more than what you've seen here."

"I know that. It's beautiful mountains, sparkling lakes, blue oceans, sandy beaches, amazing coffee, and sweet people. I never judge a place by the worst of its society. So maybe we will see each other again." She looked over and caught the chin lift from Rick before turning back to her. "Are you ready?"

Abril nodded. "Yes. Mr. Rick and Mr. Hop will fly me back to Guatemala City. They'll make sure I get to my apartment, and as you said, my life will go back to normal." She leaned in for a tight hug and added, "Normal is fine with me."

Natalie laughed at her words but felt the prick of tears sting her eyes. "Goodbye, Abril. Take care."

Separating, they walked over to the Keepers. Rick and Hop assisted Abril inside a vehicle, and Natalie waved as they disappeared down the road.

Turning to Leo, her gaze roved over his naked chest. He'd been checked out by the paramedics who were treating the other injured, but the sight of the horrific blood-red bruise over his upper left thorax made her angry all over again. Lower, and he might have a broken rib. Or if the weapon fired at him had been more powerful—

"Hey, stop thinking," he said, interrupting the thoughts taking her down the emotional path to fury again. He reached out with his right arm and snagged her close. "I'm good. We got Abril, so our mission was successful."

She lifted her hand, cupping his cheek and tracing the dimple in his chin with her thumb. "Our mission. I like the sound of that."

He held her gaze and nodded before a smile curved his lips, and she knew her heart was completely gone.

22

Deciding to go with Poole and Dolby on the boat to the dock near where they had a private plane in Mexico that had brought them down and was waiting, Leo made his way down the slope to the beach. His chest hurt like a fucker, but without the vest, he'd be dead, so he'd put up with the pain. Plus, he wasn't about to deny that Natalie's constant presence was welcome. She'd nudged her shoulder up under his armpit, and it was easy to settle his arm over her shoulders.

The mission had almost gone completely FUBAR, thanks to Alarico's duplicitous actions, but in the end, they'd managed to save Abril while keeping themselves alive at the same time. Climbing into the smaller motorboat Dolby had taken to get to Bastion's dock, he settled against the constant rocking with Natalie nestled in the crook of his arm. It only took a few minutes to get to the larger boat Poole and Dolby arrived in, and they were underway. The bouncing of the boat was uncomfortable, but he had no complaints with Natalie's body pressed against his.

If either of the other Keepers wondered about the change in relationship status between him and Nat, they kept their thoughts to themselves, for which he was grateful. The last thing he wanted was for her to become self-conscious or get scared off. Glancing down at her smile, he felt she wouldn't panic so easily.

It only took an hour to get to the dock, where he eschewed assistance getting off the boat but could not keep the grimace from his face.

"You know, every time I see you in pain, it makes me want to go right back there and kick Alarico's and Bastion's asses."

"Babe, Bastion is dead."

"Yeah, well, then I could just kick Alarico's twice!"

He chuckled and tried to hide the wince. She huffed again, and he wondered why he thought he could hide anything from her. When they arrived at the private airstrip and met the pilot, he was glad it was more than just a puddle jumper. Not that he had any problem flying in the most rudimentary aircraft, but he wanted Natalie to be comfortable. Once in the air, he wasn't surprised when she looked over and said, "We used to crack open a beer when a mission was over."

He also wasn't surprised when Dolby grinned and leaned down to an insulated bag at his feet to pull out four beers. Tossing her one, Leo didn't miss the smile that spread over her face. As the pilot flew them home, the three Keepers and the best friend he'd ever had clicked their beer cans together and drank to a successful mission.

When she finally leaned her head against his good shoulder and fell asleep, he rested his head against the top of hers, but sleep didn't come.

Every time he closed his eyes, the sight of Bastion aiming his gun toward Natalie caused his eyes to pop open again as his heart raced. He had no idea whose bullet had ended Bastion's life, but he hoped it was his. Swallowing deeply, he held her tighter and willed his heartbeat to slow.

Poole twisted his head around, his gaze drifting over them. "You okay, man?"

Thinking of what he had in his arms and the fact that they were all going home safely, he replied, "I will be."

"Told you the first time I met Natalie that she was amazing. I see nothing's changed."

"Hell, no," he agreed.

"That's not quite right," Dolby added, his eyes twinkling as he looked over his shoulder at them as well. "Seems like some things have changed."

"What took you so long?" Poole asked.

Leo considered his reply as the comforting feel of her warm body leaning against his provided the answer. "We're best friends. Everything we did and everything we were and everything we went through brought us to this point." Kissing the top of her head again, he breathed her in. "Can't rush perfection."

Poole and Dolby nodded, their smiles still in place as they settled in for the rest of the trip.

It was late in the day when they landed near LA. Dolby handed him his keys as they climbed down from the plane. "Brought your vehicle from the main airport before we left."

"Damn, thanks," he said, clasping their hands as he said goodbye. "Tell Carson I'll call him to report and talk to him. He'll understand."

Stepping back, he watched as Natalie walked over to both men, her expression sincere. "I can't thank you enough. I know you came to help Leo, but what you did for Abril and me—"

"No thanks needed," Poole said, shaking his head and pulling her in for a hug. "This is how we roll."

Dolby grinned as Poole let her go when Leo grumbled. "Get used to it," he called out as he hugged her, too, winking at Leo over her head.

Before she could ask what he meant, the two Keepers headed to their vehicle. Turning to Leo, she held out her hand.

He looked down at her palm, then lifted his gaze to her expectant face. "Sorry, babe, I don't know what you want?"

"Your keys."

His brows rose. "My keys?"

Her hand plopped onto her hip. "Are you confused or being purposely obtuse?"

"Neither. I understand you're requesting the keys to my SUV, but considering I'm driving, I don't see a need for you to have them."

Her chin jerked back, and he had to battle to hide his grin. Getting her riled up used to be a favorite pastime when they served together. Now, he began to see the fun in working together again.

"You know what," she huffed, sliding her shoulder under the armpit of his good arm as they started walking to his vehicle. "As long as you're in the car with me, I don't have to have your keys in my hand."

"What makes you think I'm going to let you drive my SUV? Hell, your legs probably don't even reach the accelerator."

He almost stumbled as she halted. Twisting her head around to look up at him, she pinched her lips together. "I would elbow you in the ribs, but considering you're injured, I'll take pity on you. But one more quip about my height—"

"What height?"

Her eyes widened a second before she burst out laughing. Clutching her stomach, she bent over, the peals of giggles overtaking her. Seeing the light in her eyes as her bright smile spread across her beautiful face was worth the threat of her elbow. Finally catching her breath, she repositioned her body to support his. "God, I needed that laugh."

"So I'm forgiven?" he asked, squeezing her waist as he allowed her to maneuver him to the passenger side. As much as he wanted to drive, he knew that with limited mobility, she would probably be the better driver at the moment.

"Of course," she grunted as she helped him in. Once she'd climbed into the driver's seat and moved the seat forward so that her foot would reach the accelerator, she looked toward him as she started the engine. "Always, Leo. Always here for you."

His chest hurt, but it had nothing to do with the injury and everything to do with the woman who held his heart in her hand.

Soon they were on the road to her apartment north of the city. Not wanting to do anything once they arrived but shower and fall into bed, she insisted on feeding him before letting him sleep, and he couldn't deny that sounded good. There was no food in her apartment since she'd been gone for over a month, so they ordered subs to be delivered.

Walking into the bathroom, he called out, "Babe, I know you'd love a bath with one of those explosions that smell so good."

She followed, laughing as they both crowded inside her tiny bathroom. "Bath explosion? You mean a bath bomb. Anyway, you should shower first."

He turned and grinned. "Nah, you go first. I'm moving slow."

"Okay, but I'll shower. I'm too grungy to sit in a bath now." Winking, she dragged a finger down his arm. "Want to join me?"

He was tempted, but considering the showerhead was over her bathtub, he figured they'd kill themselves trying to shower together. "Jesus, I hate to say no, but in that tiny thing, there's no way."

She scrunched her nose but nodded. Pulling off her boots, she then stripped off her black shirt and pants. His gaze took in the sight, and his cock jumped despite his fatigue and injury.

As he stood and listened to the water running over her naked body that was barely hidden behind the cheap shower curtain, he figured they could have made shower-sex work. Then as he peeled his clothes off and looked into the mirror, he sighed. *Or maybe not.* The wound hurt like a bitch and looked like hell, but bruises would heal.

As she stepped out, her beautiful body on display, her gaze landed on his chest, and her lips quivered until she pressed them together. Stepping closer, she placed her palm on his abs, then leaned in to settle her lips over the bruised skin, kissing him lightly.

Before he could throw sense out the window and take her to bed despite the pain, she stepped back. "Shower. Then we'll eat. Then we'll sleep."

"And then?"

Her lips curved. "And then we'll figure it out from there."

He liked that answer. A fuck of a lot. And he knew exactly how he wanted to show her how he felt.

So he showered and pulled on boxers and a T-shirt. They ate subs with chips, pickles, and beer while sitting on her sofa with his feet on the coffee table and her feet on his legs. Then they climbed into her small bed, with him on his back, and she draped over his left side. He wondered if he could sleep with the images of Bastion holding a gun on her playing over in his mind. Forcing his thoughts to the woman safe in his arms, he finally breathed easier. And then fell asleep.

When his eyes fluttered open the next morning, he

was greeted with her beautiful face peering down at him. "Hey."

She smiled, her finger tracing over his face and ending up at the dimple in his chin. "Hey, yourself." Her gaze moved down, landing on his black, blue, and red bruised chest, and her smile dropped. "How do you feel?"

It was on the tip of his tongue to say that he felt like he'd been hit by a bullet but knew she wouldn't find that funny. She'd also be able to read through any bullshit. "Stiff. Sore. But I slept like a rock, and waking up to you is the best medicine I could ever want or need."

Her smile returned, lighting her whole face. "That's a really good answer." She leaned forward, her mouth replacing her fingers as she placed little kisses over his face. Cupping her jaw, he took over the kiss, the velvet touch of her tongue on his making his cock jump.

Her gaze shot down to where the sheet had slid to his waist, and her eyes widened.

"Sorry, babe. When you're around, it has a mind of its own." He lifted her chin with his knuckle. "I hate to say this, but I'm not sure I can move the way I need to."

Biting her lip, she leaned forward, kissing his chest, then slid down to kiss his abs. His cock swelled, pressing against the sheet as though to escape its confines. She continued to kiss along his body and whatever blood was still in his brain rushed south. "Babe…"

"Let me do this, Leo. Please. I want to take care of you."

"Nat, honey… you never have to beg." His voice

sounded guttural to himself, so he could only imagine what it sounded like to her.

Her smile grew wide again as she continued her trailing kisses over his abs until her mouth opened and her lips encircled his cock. She shifted her body over his legs and began to slide her mouth up and down, alternating between sucking and licking.

His eyes would have rolled back in his head, except he didn't want to miss a moment of watching her work her magic on his body. Not just a woman. Not just any woman. But her. His Natalie. He forgot the ache from his injury as his heart beat faster.

As she bobbed up and down, her slick lips and tongue worked miracles as all thoughts left his mind other than the feel and sight of her. Just when he didn't think he could hold on longer, he managed to groan, "Ride me."

The order came from a place deep inside that wanted to come inside her but should have been ashamed that he hadn't made her come first. About to pull his words back, she straddled his hips and rose to place the tip of his cock at her entrance, her eyes bright and her smile wide. His hands found her hips, but she settled down, and all other thoughts fled his mind as her tight, slick sex sheathed his erection.

Keeping her hand on her thighs, she lifted and plunged, over and over, in a rhythm as old as time but just as new as the first time. His lower back burned, and his chest ached, but he was determined to take care of her at the same time.

His hands snaked up her torso, landing on her

breasts, cupping them as they bounced, slightly pinching her erect nipples. "Come here."

"You're awfully bossy for someone who's on the bottom," she murmured, leaning forward to allow him to suck one nipple deeply into his mouth. Enclosed in a dark curtain of her hair, she kept one hand on his good shoulder and planted the other on the mattress by his head.

"You're awfully compliant for someone who's on top," he grunted, surprised he was able to speak. Her laughter speared right through him. Then the little sounds she made as he sucked harder nearly took him over the edge.

Sliding one hand from her hips to where their bodies joined, he found her nub with his thumb and circled it before pressing, eliciting the response he wanted her to have. Her body tightened around his erection. He watched, fascinated, as a deep blush rose from her chest to her hairline, where tiny dots of perspiration shone. Her muscles tensed, and her eyes held him without wavering as her orgasm had her groaning just as his release shot from him, filling her as he pumped until the last drop.

As his cock slid from her warm channel, she dropped to his good side, her damp hair spreading out on the pillow. Their ragged breaths slowed, and it seemed to take longer for his heart to ease its pounding. *Condom.*

"Shit, babe, I never even thought about a condom. I'm clean… we get tested, and I swear I've never gone ungloved. Plus, hell, it's been a long time since I've—"

"Shhh," she whispered, placing her finger over his lips. "I'm clean, too. And God knows, I've been celibate for a while, deciding that no sex was better than always wishing I was with you instead."

He shifted, his hand coming up to cup her face. "If you get pregnant—"

"I'm on the pill, Leo. It's all good."

With legs tangled, he wrapped his arm around her, and nodded as thoughts of little Natalies or Leos filled his mind. Smiling with hopes for the future, he kissed the top of her head as her cheek lay on his shoulder. Her fingers traced over his tattoos and then made their way to feather touches over his bruises. He captured her fingers in his hand, bringing them to his mouth. "I'm okay," he assured.

She leaned her head back and held his gaze, unasked questions swarming in her eyes.

"And we're more than okay," he added. As her lips curved upward, he felt another kick in his chest. More powerful than the bullet that knocked the breath out of him. Love. He felt it… now he needed to let her know. "I love you, Natalie. Always have. But I'm also *in* love with you. The I-want-you-to-be-with-me-forever kind of *in* love."

A little gasp slipped from her lips, even more potent than the ones she'd emitted when she came. Her eyes widened at the same time her smile did. Her forefinger found his dimple again. "I love you, too. I can't remember a time when I didn't love you. And I'm *in* love with you, also. The forever kind."

He shifted, ignoring the pain as he lay facing her.

Cupping her jaw, he swept his finger over her cheek. "Will you marry me?"

She blinked, but he didn't give her a chance to speak... at least not yet.

"I know it seems fast, but babe, we've known each other for the better part of a decade. I know what you look like first thing in the morning when you've been up all night making sure our brothers and I made it through the mission safely. I know what you look like when you're made up for a night out or the way you look when you've puked your guts out after that night out. I know what you look like when you're ready to take on some shit after watching some asshole in a bar hit on an unwilling woman, and I've seen you tear up over a hurt animal. I know what your parents put you through, and I know what you'd do to protect those you love. You tie me up in knots more than any other woman I've ever met, yet you allow me the freedom to be the man I need to be. And finally, you're the best friend I've ever had. The best friend I'll ever have. And I want to go to my grave having held your hand to the end with our kids at our sides."

Her breath hitched, and she blinked, unable to keep the tears at bay. He smiled, his heart warming at the sight.

She swallowed deeply, sucked in a shuddering breath, and nodded. "You're the best friend I could have ever wanted, and as I fell more in love with you, I was terrified. Scared of changing our friendship, yet scared of eventually watching you fall for someone else and knowing that would permanently change everything between us."

"So what's your answer, Nat?"

Her lips pressed together tightly as she swallowed deeply again. He held his breath, then let it loose in a rush as she nodded and smiled.

"Yes. My answer is yes. I'll marry you."

23

ONE WEEK LATER

Natalie smiled at Tad as he rose from his chair and sputtered, his face turning an interesting color of apoplectic red. "You can't quit! Carlotta's agent called to say you informed her that you wouldn't be on her detail. I assured her that you were!"

"Sorry to make a liar out of you, but then the truth never fell easily from your lips anyway." She turned and, looking over her shoulder, winked. "See ya, Tad. You can mail my last paycheck. And don't be late or skimpy with it… I know how to get into your system and can really fuck things up if you try to fuck me over." Waggling her fingers, she walked out to his cries of, "You'll be sorry when no one else hires you!"

Stepping out onto the hot sidewalk into the LA sunshine, she slid her sunglasses down from where they'd held her hair back and placed them over her eyes. Blowing out a deep breath, she walked down the street. At the corner, she turned and smiled as her gaze landed on Leo leaning against his SUV parked on the street.

Jeans that did wonders for his thighs and ass. His biceps bulged as his arms were crossed over a tight T-shirt-covered chest. His light brown hair, a little longer on top, had her fingers itching to run through the curls. Hazel eyes always made her think of a lion ready to pounce and protect. And when his lips curved into a smile, her heart skipped a beat.

She walked straight up to him, her head leaning back farther the closer she got. His chin dipped so their gazes stayed locked together. When the toes of her shoes touched the toes of his boots, she stopped and grinned. "Howdy."

Chuckling, his eyes warmed. "Howdy, right back at you." He inclined his head toward the building she just came from. "Is it done?"

Her smile widened. "All done."

"Good." He turned and opened the door for her, waiting until she had buckled in before he shut the door and walked around the front to the driver's side. As soon as he was in, he twisted to her. "Want to go out to lunch to celebrate telling your asshole boss that you quit?"

Sucking in her lips, she tilted her head to the side and grinned. "I'd rather go back to my crappy apartment, which I might not be able to afford if I don't get another job soon, and jump into bed with you."

Leo's reflector sunglasses kept her from seeing his eyes, but she had no doubt that he blinked. Grinning, she reached out and placed her hand on his.

"Fuck, Nat. I want to drag you over the console and take you right here."

Her brow slightly lowered as she looked at the narrow space between his body and the steering wheel. "I'm not sure how that would work, big guy."

"We could get creative. But then we'd get arrested on this public street, and I'm not about to share your ass with anyone. So as much as I want you, let's get something to eat before we go back to your crappy apartment."

Her brow lowered. "Well, damn, you must be hungry." Just then, her stomach growled, and a rare giggle slipped out. While a giggle wasn't her usual sound of mirth, she'd been doing more of it in the past week. *Maybe this is what total bliss feels like.*

It didn't take long for him to make his way through traffic heading north, past the turnoff near her apartment, but he continued for another hour. He seemed to have a destination in mind, and she'd give him anything, even if her stomach rumbled. He finally turned off at a food truck parked on a gravel lookout that offered a spectacular ocean view. Not expecting fancy, she was still surprised at his choice of places to eat, considering the time it took to get there.

He met her at her door and, with his hand resting lightly on her back, escorted her to the open window of the truck, where he ordered tacos, burritos, nachos, and beer. As the server loaded up the bag, she lifted a brow. "Damn, you *are* hungry."

Laughing, he paid and carried the bag while she took the beer. He walked to the other side of the truck and said, "There's a picnic table over here."

The area was vacant, probably due to the after-lunch, pre-dinner lull in business. A single man was sitting at one of the tables, his back to them. Leo walked past the empty tables and led her over to the occupied one, setting the food down in the middle. The man turned around, a wide smile on his face as he stood to greet Leo, then looked toward her. *Carson!*

Inclining his head her way, he greeted, "Natalie. Good to see you again."

Setting the beer down quickly, she reached out her hand. "Carson, it's nice to see you also." She shot a narrow-eyed glare toward Leo, then turned back to his boss. "A surprise, but a nice surprise."

The three sat down, and Leo opened the food bags, laying everything out on the table like a buffet. For several minutes, they ate, talking companionably, but she had no doubt the planned lunch was much more than a friendly get-together.

Leo bussed the table when the food was gone, tossing the trash into a nearby can. Her gaze followed him as he moved to sit at another table by himself. Turning to Carson, she waited. This was their show, and she was willing to let it play out and not make any assumptions.

Carson held her gaze. "I owe you an apology for placing trust in Alarico. If I had known—"

"No, sir– Carson. You have nothing to apologize for. We all went with the intel we had at the time. Not all intel is good or right, but we make do."

His gaze didn't waver, then he slowly nodded. "Your work in Guatemala was good. Excellent, in fact."

Her lips twitched. "I assume you're not referring to my Carlotta guard duties."

Chuckling, he shook his head. "No, although I'm sure those were excellent, as well."

She smiled in return. "Thank you."

"You're cool under pressure. Think fast on your feet. I'd heard you were tops at analyzing intel but have now had a chance to see it for myself. You understand mission development and changes. Confidentiality. Dedication. The desire to protect. Camaraderie. Others before self."

"You keep going, and I just might get a big head." The flippant words left her mouth before she thought them through, and she scrunched her nose in regret. "Sorry."

Carson lifted a brow. "I talked to your former boss."

At that, she blanched. *Well, fuck... what the hell would Tad say about me—*

"Not Mr. Thaddeus Jones of Titus Bodyguard Services."

The air rushed from her lungs. "Thank God. I'm not sure he'd have anything good to say about me on a great day, and considering I just quit with a threat that he'd better not fuck me over on my last paycheck, I'm sure I'm not his favorite person."

Carson's lips quirked, and while she didn't look over at the other table, she could have sworn that she heard Leo snort.

"I talked to Colonel Burnley. The last CO you had while serving as an ACE support team member."

At the mention of one of the toughest commanders

she'd ever known, as well as one of her favorite and most respected, she breathed a little easier.

"He had nothing but the highest praise for you. In fact, he said you were the best, and when sending out a team, he always wanted you for support, knowing he had a better chance of getting them all back in one piece with the mission accomplished."

She blinked, hit by the sudden and inappropriate desire to cry. Swallowing deeply, she nodded and cleared her throat. "That's good to hear. Thank you, sir."

He nodded. "Carson."

"Thank you, Carson," she repeated, still wondering where all this was going. Leo had previously talked to her about working at LSI-WC, but she hadn't considered it further. Nothing had been said about it since they'd come back from Guatemala. *But then, with Leo's recuperation, they'd hardly left her bed.* And she'd never be so bold as to pursue the idea, considering an offer would have to come from Carson.

Her palms began to sweat, and she placed them on her thighs, trying to wipe them without making it look like that was what she was doing. After all, he'd said she was cool under pressure. *With my armpits soaking right now, I'm far from cool.* Blanking her expression, she waited not-so-patiently. If he was going to tell her that he wasn't hiring now, or that he didn't think she'd be a fit, or it would be weird since she was dating Leo—

Leo turned around and looked at her, a question on his face. Jerking her gaze back to Carson, he appeared to be waiting. "Oh… shit… I'm sorry."

"Christ, Nat," Leo said, his eyes wide. "You want to answer him or just keep us all hanging?"

Swinging her head back, feeling like she was watching a ping-pong match, she blurted, "Can you repeat the question?" Seeing his raised brows, she continued to blab. "It's just that I was lost… wondering what was happening here and all the reasons what I hoped for probably wasn't going to happen, and my mind just… uh… shit. I'm sorry, Carson."

He chuckled again. "I've also been told you're completely honest. Gotta tell you, that's another reason for making you the perfect candidate to become a Keeper. My question was this—are you interested in coming to work for LSI-WC as a mission analyst for starters, and then with more training, you could become involved in active missions if that's something you'd be amenable to?"

The air suddenly felt thin. The desire to fist pump her excitement battled with the feeling that she might faint. Fainting would not look good for a badass, so she straightened her spine and held his gaze. "Yes. I can absolutely say that it would be an honor to work for LSI-WC and become a Keeper."

Leo stood and walked to their table, sliding onto the bench next to her. She twisted her head around to peer up at him, smiling at the gleam in his eyes from the reflected light off the ocean. Not willing to kiss him in front of her new boss, she simply winked before turning back to Carson.

"This means a lot to me, Carson. I promise you will always receive my best."

He reached across the table and took her smaller hand in his for a warm shake. "That's all I can ask of any of us." He shifted his gaze between her and Leo. "There was a time when I'd never consider hiring the significant other of one of my employees, assuming it was a recipe for disaster. But Leo, here, convinced me to give Jeannie a chance with his relationship 101 advice. Glad I listened to him. And not too long ago, I gave him some relationship advice in return. Glad he finally listened to me."

With that, he stood, and they took to their feet, as well. "Come in one day this week and meet the others formally. With your security clearance still in effect, you can get started as soon as Rachel sets you up with the employment paperwork."

"I'll be there tomorrow." She didn't care that she might sound desperate. Sure, she needed a paycheck now that she had quit, but mostly she just wanted to jump into the new job.

With a grin and a chin lift, Carson said goodbye. She let out a long breath and whispered, "Did that just happen?"

Leo slid his arm over her shoulders and squeezed. "Yeah, babe, it did."

Twisting her head around and up, she peered into his face. "Did you arrange this? I mean, talk him into hiring me?" Her gaze never left his. If she could count on one thing in this world, it was Leo. And he'd never lie to her. Ever.

He shifted so they faced each other and took her hands in his, placing them lightly over his heart. "Babe, I swear that Carson had mentioned you working for him from the moment he first met you when you came to visit me after I was hired. I'd told him how you deserved to be happy in your work but that you feared our friendship might suffer. Now, I'm certain that you and I are not only best friends but soul mates, teammates, fellow Keepers, and nothing will ever get in the way."

Her heart pounded as the air between them crackled. "Do you remember when I said earlier that I wanted to take you to bed and jump you? Well, I still do. Actually, even more than I did then, which is almost impossible."

His eyes darkened, and she stared, fascinated by the twitch in his jaw. "I love you, Nat, but fuck… you can't say things like that and not expect me to act."

Reaching up to touch his dimple, she grinned. "Oh, I do expect you to do something about it—ooph!" He scooped her up into his arms. "You can't do this! You're hurt."

He dropped a glare toward her. "Woman, don't tell me that you want to jump me and then expect me to worry about being hurt."

She didn't have time to retort before he threw open his SUV door and placed her into the passenger seat. When he pulled onto the highway heading north, she looked over. "Where are we going?"

"My place is closer." He reached over and clasped her hand.

He kept her hand in his, and she grinned the whole way to where he lived. He jerked into the parking space of his end-unit condo and threw open his door, stalking around the front. She unbuckled and had barely gotten her hand on the handle when it was wrenched from her grip. Leo bent again, his arms scooping her up and against his chest.

Remembering his earlier words, she kept her mouth closed as he carried her to the door. She'd been there numerous times, but this time, it felt different. As he set her feet on the floor, she hesitated. As always, Leo noticed everything about her.

"You okay, Nat?"

She nodded, pressing her lips together. "Yeah. It's just that this will be the first time we're in your place since..."

"Since...?"

"You know. Since we became a couple. It feels different entering your place now."

"Not my place."

She blinked, her head tilting to the side. "What do you mean it's not your place?"

He leaned down, but with his sunglasses still on, she couldn't see his eyes. "Not just *my* place. Think of it as yours also. Anyway, you'll be getting rid of that shithole apartment so you might as well get used to being at my place until we find something together."

She felt the air rush out as her lips curved. "Our place."

"Yeah, babe. Our place."

She wasn't sure she could drag the air back into her lungs but didn't want to pass out before experiencing all that was Leo in his kick-ass condo. *Our kick-ass condo.* Oh, there would be discussions, probably loud ones, about his high-handed lunch arrangement with Carson and declaring his place to now be theirs, but at the moment, all she could think of was Leo, her, a bed, and being naked. Inclining her head toward the door, she lifted her brow. "You gonna get this door open?"

He held her gaze for a second, then growled. Literally growled. She'd never orgasmed from a man's voice before, but it hit her that she just might right now. He unlocked the door, swung it open, and ushered her inside. She wondered if he was going to carry her to bed, but he stopped as her gaze took in the space she was so familiar with. *Nothing has changed, yet everything is different.*

He reached up and slid his sunglasses off, tossing them to the table nearby. Then he repeated the action with her sunglasses. Now, with nothing between their gazes, she could see the intensity in his eyes. "Yeah, you're right," he agreed. "We're the same, but now, even better."

She hadn't realized she'd spoken aloud but should have known that he would get it. Get her. Get them. Lifting on her toes, she balanced with her hands on his shoulders and placed a kiss on his lips. "I've wanted to do this forever... kiss you at your place." Touching her lips to his again, she added, "In fact, I've dreamed about it for a long time."

His arms banded around her, pulling her close. As he took over the kiss, it flamed hot and wild. Just the way she liked it. And when he lifted her, she wrapped her legs around his waist as he carried her toward the bedroom. *Oh yeah... sometimes dreams really do come true.*

24

THREE MONTHS LATER

"If you can get to the bridge at the end of the town where the river divides, you can make it to where Hop will be waiting. There's no threat on the radar from there," Natalie reported, her gaze not straying from the computer screen in front of her in the LSI-WC compound at the back of the decommissioned light-house Carson had purchased on the coast of California.

Leo looked over her shoulder at the screen, seeing the information she was feeding to Bennett, who'd run into a few problems with his security detail. Jeb had pulled up the satellite images, but it was Natalie who could take the images and, with almost no time or prep, analyze the incoming intel and offer the logistics needed.

Looking over at Carson, he grinned before swinging his gaze to the other Keepers in the room, knowing they each appreciated Natalie now working alongside them.

The tense minutes passed, and Bennett successfully

escorted the medical company CEO through an unfriendly crowd after a political meeting, radioing in that he was now with Hop and they would be flying out soon. Letting out an audible sigh, Natalie leaned back in her chair, then swiveled around, looking up at Leo. Then she smiled.

And just like all her smiles, it hit him right in his gut. He was just about to congratulate her when Rick walked in with his face contorted in a grimace. Surprised at his easygoing friend's expression, he asked, "What's up, man?"

Rick plopped down into a chair and then scrubbed his hand over his face. "It's Abbie. Blake's sister."

Leo had met William Blake, one of Mace's original LSI Keepers in Maine. With Rick's brother also an original Keeper, Rick had met Abbie when she'd visited. From what Rick had said, Abbie planned to join Mace's team but then accepted another CIA special op that took her to Cairo, Egypt. He'd never asked if Rick and she had hooked up, but listening to Rick talk about her, he figured something was there. Rick had decided to move to California to work with LSI-WC, and Leo also wondered if Abbie had anything to do with that.

"What's going on?" he asked.

"Don't know. She and I have occasionally talked since she's been in Cairo, but now she's gone silent. I get it, you know. Working CIA ops means she can't always be in contact. But I just got a call from my brother asking if I'd spoken to her recently. Rank knows that she and I are friends, but to be honest, I have no idea if Blake knows. Anyway, it seems he's worried. It's probably nothing, but I'd like this assignment to be over for her. At least, if she's in Maine working for Mace, I'll know she's safe."

"If you're needed, you only have to ask," Carson said. "She's one of us, even if she's connected to Maine LSI."

"Thanks, boss. I appreciate it."

Rick turned back to his station, but Natalie glanced up at Leo, shot him a smile, then walked over to Rick. "Come on, big guy. Bennett and Hop are safe and on their way home. The rest of us are finished unless Carson has something else on the books. It's time to hit the bar after work. Leo and I are going, so come with us."

Carson added, "Jeannie and I will come, too. And if I know her, she'll get Rachel and Teddy to join us."

Leo watched with pride as Natalie squeezed Rick's shoulder until he turned and grinned before standing.

"Who are you texting?" Leo asked as they drove to the bar.

Natalie's fingers continued to fly over her phone as she replied, "Abril."

"She still coming to the wedding?"

"She'd better! She's a bridesmaid! Hell, if it wasn't for her friendship, and now Jeannie and Rachel, I'd be standing up in front of the minister alone with you and your whole entourage of *alpha besties*, and I'd look like a loser!"

Laughter erupted as he pulled into the parking lot.

Turning off the engine, he shifted to face her. Lifting a brow, he repeated, "Alpha besties? What the fuck is that?"

"Oh, don't pretend you don't know. You and all the Keepers."

"Babe… they're your friends, too."

"Yeah, but they'd look stupid in bridesmaid dresses!"

Still laughing, he shook his head. "Our wedding will be fucking epic no matter who's in a dress." She was quiet, and he sobered. "Are you okay?"

She crinkled her nose and sighed. "Are you sure we can't just grab a justice of the peace and head to town hall?"

He reached over to cup her face, his large hand cradling her cheek. "No. You deserve everything I can give you."

She leaned her head into his hand, and her eyes fluttered closed for a few seconds before popping open again. "You're just afraid of your mom having a fit if we don't get married in a church."

"Damn right, I'm afraid of my mom!"

She huffed, but he knew it was for show as her lips curved upward.

"But anyway, back to Abril. Yes, she's flying in several days ahead of schedule. She has her passport and paperwork, and the ticket has already been bought. Hop will pick her up at the airport and bring her here. I figured since she'd met him, he'd be a good choice."

"Is she still doing okay?"

Nodding, Natalie smiled. "Loves her job. She's already assigned to another movie filming crew, but they won't start until she returns from her trip to the States." Cutting her eyes away before bringing them back had Leo suspicious.

"What do you have up your sleeve?"

"Nothing!" After a few more seconds of his narrow-eyed glaring, she crinkled her nose again. "Okay, fine. I told her that we'd plan a trip to the coast of Guatemala to have a beach resort vacation next summer. I figure that we can lounge in the sun, and I get to see her again."

He chuckled, then leaned forward, his hand still holding her face. Kissing her, lightly at first and then sliding his tongue inside her mouth, he felt the punch he always felt when they were together.

"Come on!" a loud shout came from nearby.

Jerking apart, they spied the others walking through the parking lot toward the bar. Natalie flipped them off, earning laughter from the other Keepers and a head-shake from Leo. "Let's go, tiger."

Climbing down from his SUV, they fell in step with Teddy and Rachel as they walked together. He felt Natalie tense next to him before she suddenly stopped and blurted, "Teddy?"

The burly man turned and smiled at her. "Yes, darlin'?"

Leo held his breath, having an idea of what she was thinking but uncertain how it would play out.

She sucked in a deep breath and said, "I was going to ask you something. But you can say no. I mean, it'd be fine. It's not like you need to—"

"Babe," Leo whispered, seeing Teddy's brow crease. "Ask."

She nodded, and the words rushed from her lips. "I wanted to know if you'd walk me down the aisle. But, seriously, you don't—"

Teddy's arms jerked out and encircled her, pulling her from Leo's side. "Oh damn, girl! It would be an honor!"

"Really?" she squeaked as he held her tightly.

Leo fought and lost the battle to hide his grin as he looked from them to the stalwart Rachel, who appeared to blink back tears, something he never thought he'd see.

"Hell yeah, Natalie," Teddy enthused. "I'm honored you'd ask, and I'm honored to say yes!"

Natalie's shoulders relaxed as she moved back to Leo's side, and he pulled her close. As the four of them walked inside, she peered up and admitted, "This wedding shit is harder than I thought it would be."

Laughing, he bent to place a G-rated kiss on her lips, not willing to give anyone else a show. He slung his arm around her shoulders, and they made their way through the tables toward the back, where the others had settled around a large table. She moved to sit next to Jeannie, and he noted Rachel was just across from them. The three women immediately leaned their heads together, and he heard the words *flowers, cake, reception, and even dresses* floating between them. Words he never thought he'd hear her say with excitement and enthusiasm.

"I don't care what Leo's mom is doing. I've got the bridesmaids, our luncheon, our spa day, and our part of the reception," Jeannie declared. "As soon as Abril gets here, we'll all head to the hotel I've booked."

"And I'm going to handle the flowers," Rachel said, her tone brooking no argument.

Natalie blew out a long, shaky breath. "Oh God, this is so over my head."

"That's why you have us," Jeannie said, smiling widely. "And I'm so excited to help you plan!"

Natalie's smile beamed, and he pulled her closer, his fingertips tracing over her shoulders. He relaxed, his heart filling as the woman he loved had finally found and embraced a sisterhood she deserved.

Several hours later, and a few beers in, Natalie leaned over. "Have you noticed that Rick isn't chasing skirts? Think this might have something to do with Abbie?"

Leo stared into her bright eyes, and like always, his heart raced. "Don't know. Figure we'll find out some-time along the way. But maybe they're just friends."

Her dark eyes flared. "You know what can happen with best friends, right?"

He smiled but remained silent, waiting to see what she would say.

She touched his dimple and grinned. "They fall in love."

Leaning closer until his lips were a whisper away from her ear, he blew a breath across her cheek. "Yeah, babe. You and me. Friends who fell in love."

Then his lips glided to her mouth, and he kissed her. His best friend. His Nat.

Don't miss the next LSIWC Keepers!

Rick

Hop

And don't forget the next Baytown Hero!

Finding a Hero

Finding a Hero

For all of Miss Ethel's boys:

Heroes at Heart (Military Romance)

Zander

Rafe

Cael

Jaxon

Jayden

Asher

Zeke

Cas

Lighthouse Security Investigations

Mace

Rank

Walker

Drew

Blake

Tate

Levi

Clay

Cobb

Bray

Josh

Knox

Lighthouse Security Investigations West Coast

Carson

Leo

Rick

Hop

Hope City (romantic suspense series co-developed

with Kris Michaels

Brock book 1

Sean book 2

Carter book 3

Brody book 4

Kyle book 5

Ryker book 6

Rory book 7

Killian book 8

Torin book 9

Blayze book 10

Griffin book 11

Saints Protection & Investigations

(an elite group, assigned to the cases no one else wants…or
can solve)

Serial Love

Healing Love

Revealing Love

Seeing Love

Honor Love

Sacrifice Love

Protecting Love

Remember Love

Discover Love

Surviving Love

Celebrating Love

Searching Love

Follow the exciting spin-off series:

Alvarez Security (military romantic suspense)

Gabe

Tony

Vinny

Jobe

SEALs

Thin Ice (Sleeper SEAL)

SEAL Together (Silver SEAL)

Undercover Groom (Hot SEAL)

Also for a Hope City Crossover Novel / Hot SEAL…

A Forever Dad

Long Road Home

Military Romantic Suspense

Home to Stay (a Lighthouse Security Investigation crossover novel)

Home Port (an LSI West Coast crossover novel)

Letters From Home (military romance)

Class of Love

Freedom of Love

Bond of Love

The Love's Series (detectives)

Love's Taming

Love's Tempting

Love's Trusting

The Fairfield Series (small town detectives)

Emma's Home

Laurie's Time

Carol's Image

Fireworks Over Fairfield

Please take the time to leave a review of this book. Feel free to contact me, especially if you enjoyed my book. I love to hear from readers!

Facebook

Email

Website

ABOUT THE AUTHOR

I am an avid reader of romance novels, often joking that I cut my teeth on the historical romances. I have been reading and reviewing for years. In 2013, I finally gave into the characters in my head, screaming for their story to be told. From these musings, my first novel, Emma's Home, The Fairfield Series was born.

I was a high school counselor having worked in education for thirty years. I live in Virginia, having also lived in four states and two foreign countries. I have been married to a wonderfully patient man for forty-one years. When writing, my dog or one of my four cats can generally be found in the same room if not on my lap.

Please take the time to leave a review of this book. Feel free to contact me, especially if you enjoyed my book. I love to hear from readers!

Facebook
Email
Website

Made in the USA
Las Vegas, NV
08 September 2022

54887865R00173